A WYATT
BOOK *for*

W

—ST.—
MARTIN'S
PRESS

ELENA OF THE STARS

C. P. ROSENTHAL

A Wyatt Book
for St. Martin's Press
New York

Design by Jaye Zimet

Library of Congress
   Cataloging-in-Publication Data

Rosenthal, Chuck.
    Elena of the stars / C. P.
Rosenthal.
       p. cm.
    "A Wyatt book for St. Martin's
Press."
    ISBN 0-312-14592-6
    1. Human-animal relationships—
Wyoming—Fiction. 2. Horses—
Wyoming—Fiction.   3. Girls—
Wyoming—Fiction. I. Title.
PS3568.08368E44   1996
813'.54—dc20   96-19628
                        CIP

First A Wyatt Book for St. Martin's
Press Paperback Edition: October 1996

10 9 8 7 6 5 4 3 2

For my Marlena of the Stars

and for Gail

ACKNOWLEDGMENTS

My thanks to Bob Wyatt for his vision and insight, and to Anne Edelstein for her encouragement and perseverance over the years.

*Some say love is like
smoke, beyond all repair.*

—Leonard Cohen
"Ballad of a Runaway Horse"

EARTH AND HEAVEN

Elena's grandfather came rowing across
the river in a boat. Steering against the
current, the brown prow pushing pro-
phetically across the deep, green river.
Above her the Wyoming summer sky stretched out,
almost yellow and almost blue. She felt the winter
constellations behind that sea of air. On summer
nights a winged horse rode at the very top of the darkness and her mind filled him in between the stars. He
was so deep gray that he was almost blue, and the only
way to find him was by the stars in his wings, his head,
his hooves, his mane.

At twelve, almost thirteen, everything was a
mystery to her—the earth, the sky, her own body, and
the bodies and lives of the people around her—her
father and her mother, everyone and everything she
did not want to become.

She wanted to be the wind, or this river, or

something wild on the Tetons beyond. Something that moved across the sky or the land or the water. She did not want to be in school. She did not want to be in love. She wanted to move and move and always move, always, while everything, everyone around her wanted to stop her, contain her. Everything, everyone, said, "Stay. Stay here with me. Be here with me. Be like me."

Even her mother, who said to her, "Go. Do what you want. Do anything. Be anything." Her mother said a woman could not rely on beauty, because beauty fades. And she watched her mother, who was still beautiful and who did not rely on it, mourn the passing of her beautiful face. A woman cannot rely on children, her mother said, because your children leave you. But at night she heard her mother whisper at her bedside, hidden by the dark, her voice a prayer saying, "Never leave me, my darling, never leave me."

Her mother moved from one job to another, wrote one book after another, keeping them all alive. She lived on the verge of recognition, on the edge of fame.

And her father, who lived in dreams, who taught her the sky. Who knew what he once was? He fought in some war. He taught in some schools. He wrote some books that no one had ever seen. And he held her in this vise: "If you want a good horse, give it a large pasture."

"How large?" she said to him.

So they brought her here, to Wyoming, to her mother's father, who had run away from everything. They brought her here so she, Elena, could learn about running away.

"I don't want to learn anything," she said.

"Then don't learn anything," her father said.

And her mother looked at him in that way that

said both "Don't talk down to her" and "Don't talk on her level," and her father stopped short in his freedom and smiled.

"Tell me what to be," she said to them.

So they brought her here. Her grandfather crossed the river that was greener than the grass. The Wyoming wind hissed across the chaparral. The sky moved, its clouds like herds of horses, hooves thundering.

Joe, her grandfather, came ashore. He shook her father's hand. He hugged her mother, who cried. He took Elena's things and put them in the boat. "I'll call you in a week," he said. He pointed to the lonely phone line that came in from nowhere and disappeared over the hill on the other side of the river, the place where he had his cabin, his barn, his corral.

She knew he had no electricity, that he heated with wood, that it got cold at night here even in the summer. She knew that after the Korean War Joe lived in Japan and did not want to come back, and that his wife, her mother's mother, had been a cowgirl, a barrel racer, and that he'd traveled with her until she died, and that somewhere out here he had buried her illegally under the sage, under the forever rolling Wyoming hills.

He held Elena in front of him. "My God," he said. "My God."

"Can you row?" he said.

"Yes."

As she got in the boat her grandfather turned to her parents and said, "It's okay. Get in the car. I'll see you." And she saw their faces as she rowed, as if they were looking through rain or darkness or memory or fog, something there in their faces, something she did not understand, giving up everything.

Her grandfather let her row, even as the river pushed the boat far downstream. Though his hands were weathered, his hair gray beneath his worn brown cowboy hat, he did not look like an old man to her. He was strong. His eyes had sympathy and hunger in them.

"I'm messing up," she said.

And he said, "We'll have to walk farther then, that's all."

6

On the other side they grabbed her sleeping bag, clothes, and travel bag from the boat and carried them through the chaparral and over the hill. Now, above the river, she could smell last night's rain. On the mountains, clouds of mist rose under the gray slate cliffs and burned up under the prairie sun. The plain stretched in front of her, rolling and rolling, and her grandfather's ranch, a cabin and barn, sat starkly, simply, breaking up nothing, like black stones.

Then she saw the wild horses on the hill above, rolling like thick smoke, their hooves thumping. She felt the earth beneath her because of them. Something hot and sweet came through the air. She could not have imagined their weight, their speed, their bodies flying in a thick swarm of power over the ridge and down.

"Are they yours?" she asked.

"No," the old man said.

"Do they stay?"

"Somewhat," he said. "I have my own. They're in the corral." He pointed toward the barn, where she saw the four red horses, stirring now with the herd above them, their heads raised as they circled against the fence. "Sometimes we go out and run with them."

"With the wild ones?" she said. "With the wild horses?" Now she saw herself moving with them, running, moving fast and nowhere.

From the ranch two dogs came running and she knelt to them as they pawed her and licked at her face.

The old man watched her. He hadn't seen her for over six years, and in that time it seemed a world had passed.

She knew some of the usual things. Basic math. Some geometry and algebra. She read well enough; knew the continents, the difference between North Africa and South, North America and South, eastern Europe and west. She knew the countries of Asia.

She'd learned karate, Korean Tang Soo-Do. Ballet. The movements of the earth, the moon, the planets and stars. She could shoot a layup with either hand off the correct foot. She'd learned that art was not pictures and poems did not have meanings. And she wished she hadn't learned these things because they made her different from her friends and smarter than boys.

She had been to Mexico City, where her mother, researching the life and death of a famous poet, Sor Juana Inés de la Cruz, almost died of amoebic dysentery. She saw the great pyramids of Teotihuacán there, the ruins of Tenochtitlán, and the Basilica built under the hill where the Virgin of Guadalupe appeared, constructed from the stones of the wrecked temple of the mother goddess, Tonatzin. All of Mexico City, her mother said, was built from Aztec stones.

Elena was only a child then, and though her own mother, by way of Elena's grandmother now dead and buried somewhere here in the hills, was part mestiza, Elena's light brown hair, bleached by Los Angeles sun, was gold enough that the other children, the Mexican children, came to her to touch her hair.

She knew that the Spanish brought the horses here. That they discovered nothing, ruined everything, but that they brought the horses, and that the Mexican children who touched her hair were the sons and daughters of something she could not name but stood at the center of everything, like the stars behind the top of the noon sky.

She'd learned Spanish from Mexico and her mother, and from her father some French.

Her mother had once told her to live her life as if she were choosing her heaven. Who would she spend time with after death? Her mother chose Sor Juana, Shakespeare, Federico García Lorca.

Her father told her not to plan her life on how she guessed she might succeed, but with what she could live with having failed.

But she could not think of living at all, could not think of heaven at all, or failure or success, but only running and running.

That night she dreamed of the wild horses. And the moon, after midnight, rose full over the hillside, and drew her blood.

Her grandfather did not read poems like her mother or stories like her father, nor history, philosophy, archaeology, astronomy. His few books were about imprinting and training horses, the local birds and plants. He did not even have a radio. He had a wooden pan flute, a harmonica, a guitar. On the walls he hung woven blankets, the skulls of horses and cattle, and a black-and-white photograph that must have been of her grandmother, galloping full out on a quarter horse as they came upon a barrel.

She wore jeans and boots, a wide hat, her hair and scarf sailing behind. Even in black and white the horse looked golden, the color of her grandmother's hair. The color of Elena's hair. The animal had a dark mane and tail.

The camera had caught him in the air, as if they

were flying, the dust beneath them rising from his fury, the cowgirl above leaning upon him inseparably; not a single hoof, not the slightest part of either of them, woman or horse, touched the ground.

"I want to ride like that," she told her grandfather at a breakfast of raisin toast and black tea. They ate at a small wooden table, the window, like the rest of the kitchen, looking out to the corral and the chestnut red horses.

"Did you sleep okay?" he said to her. "You know, when you get older you don't sleep so well."

"I heard you up," she said. She had ridden some when she was little. A friend of her parents owned a stable in Oxnard. She learned English, how to post at a trot, fast and slow. She'd been tossed, bucked off on a trail ride. This he must have known. "I want to ride like Grandma."

He got up. He went to the window and watched the horses. The sun came delicately onto the window edge and everything stayed like that until the light began to come through and make a patch on the floorboards. A tabby cat emerged from somewhere and lay down in the patch of sun on the kitchen floor.

"The dogs eat rats, too," her grandfather said, "but a cat can go where a dog can't."

"I like cats," she said. They had half a dozen at home, three of them her father's and three hers. She went to the tabby, who rolled on her back when the girl touched her. The cat was thin with wiry fur like a goat. "Females are better mousers," the girl said.

"Follow me a minute," her grandfather said, and she went with him outside to another corral behind the barn. There stood the big, yellow horse with the black tail and black mane. He snorted when he saw them. Something rolled in his throat and he lifted back on his hind legs, pulling his forelegs into the air and spinning. His tail flashed.

"Think of riding a thousand-pound cat," said her grandfather. The animal came to them, throwing his legs out, stomping, then lowering his head. His nostrils twitched at the air between them. Then he pulled away, prancing.

"Well, he's more stubborn than a cat," Joe said.

"Was he Grandma's?" said Elena.

"Oh, once," said her grandfather. "For a little while."

They spent the day riding bareback. She wanted to ride in a Western saddle, but her grandfather told her that riding was all in her legs, in her body, in the shifting of her weight, that an animal who weighed a half-ton or more, who was born to run and not be ridden, could not be controlled by a bit or rein. "It's cooperation," he said. "If you get out in the hills and you're lost, none of these horses will take you in the wrong direction, even if you try to force them."

"What will they do?" Elena said.

"They'll throw you off."

"And how do they know I'm lost?" she laughed.

"How do you know you're lost?" Joe said.

The girl leaned forward and hugged her horse's neck. "Silly," she said.

"Don't hug her till you're done riding," said

her grandfather. "Everything she knows, you tell her with how you move on her back, how you tighten your legs, how you sit, lean. Be too kind during a ride and she'll be riding you."

"If they know so much," Elena said, "what do I need to know?"

Her grandfather watched her move on the animal, fearless, completely relaxed. She leaned back, her feet almost touching the animal's neck and her hair grazing its rump, then sat up.

"Well," said her grandfather, "you're good with animals. Some people are good with animals."

"Are you?"

"Not so good. Not naturally." He watched his granddaughter move up on the horse's neck as the animal broke immediately into a canter. Elena held its mane, laughing. She pulled up, her weight shifting left, and the horse turned back. She catapulted past him, her hair flying behind her. "Not like you," he said, though he knew she could not hear him. "Not like her."

In the afternoon Joe took his two rifles from the rack in the kitchen. One had a scope and a strap and he put it over his shoulder. He cradled the other in his arm as he walked with Elena over the ridge, down a gully and up again, into the Wyoming nothingness. Around a bend they came upon three antelope, their white, puffy butts bounding away into the stillness. When they stopped, Elena heard her own breath, then her grandfather's, then the wind.

At the top of the next ridge, in the distance, she could see the ruins of an old ranch with some crumbling wooden barns and broken fences.

"Some kind of fundamentalists," Joe said. "They brought, I don't know, extra wives out here, something." He looked at her. "Do you know what I'm talking about?"

"Yes," she said, though barely. "Mom lived in Salt Lake for five years." Before she was born.

"Regular Mormons don't do that anymore," said her grandfather. He watched the girl, her soft features against the sky, her hair blown by the wind, her T-shirt stretched across her breasts. Everything changed with a girl, once you had your own daughter, your own girl child. Then, suddenly, the liberties and indiscretions of men became unimaginable sins. How well did he know her? Not well.

"Your mom," he tested the girl. "What name does she go by now?" When his daughter was younger she used Margo, a variation of Margaret, her real name. He remembered during the Vietnam years when she hated him, and her mother as well, first for his traveling, then his wife's, and because he was loyal to an oil company and cared about money. She changed her first name to Gala, and her last to Ray, the surname of her first husband. Then she divorced and married again. She married Harlan Tiburon, who fought in the war. She had Elena and she kept the name Ray. Gala Ray.

"She doesn't use Gala anymore," the girl said. "She uses Calamity."

"That's right," Joe laughed. "Calamity Ray." The name that launched her career as a cowgirl humorist.

The girl laughed, too.

"Well," he said, "she's come full around."

"Not really," said Elena.

Who did not realize that he lived out here now on Social Security, on a reduced pension from an early retirement that his corporation forced on him after thirty years of loyalty, and on a savings account fed by cowgirl poet Calamity Ray. He had come around, too.

"Mormons pioneered a lot of this land," the girl's grandfather said. "Brigham Young got to Salt Lake, he just drew quadrants on a map, sent 'em out to populate the West. But you can't live in some of these places."

"You do," she said.

"I'm not raising a family."

He knelt on one knee and took the scoped rifle from his shoulder. He snapped a clip into it, then snapped a second clip into the other rifle. They were both Ruger .22s.

"This is all you need to stay alive," he said. "A horse, this little rifle, a good knife, water."

"Matches," she said.

"Maybe."

She stood dumfounded when he offered her the gun.

"You can't kill an animal with a karate chop," he said, "unless you're a lot faster than I think you are."

She took the rifle from him. She liked the warmth of the wood and the cool of the blue barrel, the smell of the fresh gun oil. He showed her how to load the clip, release the safety, place the butt on her shoulder, set the gun sights, prepare for the small kick when the firearm went off. He pointed out a rock not too far away.

"Squeeze," he said. "Don't jerk. Exhale. Then squeeze."

The wood felt warm on her cheek. She felt the recoil of the gun almost before the snap of rifle fire broke the air. It was a good-size rock and she was pretty close, but she hit it. She was proud to hit it. Though she could not imagine shooting at a living thing, still, she loved the feeling of striking at a distance.

She saw herself standing in the open prairie, the daylight caving in around her as she found the emerging stars in the gun sight, picking them out of the twilight before they could even shine, knocking the light out of the light with her desire.

In the evening they fed the horses. First the sorrels, the white diamonds on their foreheads shining in the low sun. They snorted and pawed the ground, following Joe intensely with their heads, circling until he threw the baled hay into the corral.

Then the yellow stallion. He circled, running the fence, leaning hard against the fence like a wind, his head moving out toward the plains. He held it cocked as he ran, his head above and outside the last rung of the corral, his body within.

He stood at the far end of the outdoor pen as Joe lay the grass in.

"Let's go," he said.

"I want to watch him," said Elena.

"He won't eat in front of you," her grandfather said to her. "He'd have to lower his head."

For their supper Joe broke up jerky, which he mixed with rice, and they shared beer that he kept cold in an eddy of the Green River. Elena did not like beer, but she liked drinking beer, as well as the smell of bourbon on her grandfather's breath, which mixed with the lingering aroma of smoke from the wood-stove, of smoke from a cigar or pipe or strong ciga-rettes, something, she could tell, that he smoked but had not shown her.

Tomorrow, he told her, they would tack the horses with Western bridles and saddles. After dinner she went outside. He waited quite a while, then fol-lowed her into the night. A cold, black night with wind-whipped stars.

He found her in the barn and silently watched her running her hands over the saddles, smelling the leather, making it squeak in her hands. The yellow stallion watched from his corral. The stallion peered into his paddock and into the barn at the girl, seeing something, and feeling in that narrow, deep, equine memory something in his chest that rumbled with loss and desire. There, in a vise of eyes, the girl stood on a precipice of her own nameless feelings.

Her grandfather saw the horse watching her. The girl went to the paddock and the animal stepped in, the steam rising from his back and pushing from his nostrils, like a dragon, she thought, like something from a fairy tale. He lowered his head slightly, shyly. He was so close now, so huge. She held her breath when he came to her and touched her hand. That was all. She did nothing more. And when he backed away, something rolled through him like thunder.

Elena was a strong girl. Strong enough so that in the morning, when they saddled up two of the sorrel mares, she could cinch the saddle on her own. She walked the mare until it exhaled its bloat, then tightened the saddle, grabbed the mane, and was up.

They both wanted to go, the horse and the girl. Joe made them walk. "Heels down," he said. "Elbows in. Weight back." But there were the hundred things you could not teach that she already knew. She was gentle with the bit, yet confident, firm, smooth, and the animal beneath her tried to please her. By afternoon she cantered the ring and plucked flags from the barrels on a fly.

He shot a rabbit before sunset and showed her how to skin and gut it. They ate it that night stewed in carrots and potatoes that he grew in a small garden behind the house.

That night Elena climbed the hill above the river. The moon was yet to rise from behind the slate cliffs and the sky throbbed with stars. Her thighs ached from spreading across the horse's back, her calves were still giddy from the stretch of lowering her heels into the stirrups. She felt lonely. She wished the pain would never go away.

When the quarter moon slipped above the cliffs, the hard, bright starlight softened. The sky became tender with frail light. Behind her, the snow-capped Tetons tipped the moonlight back upon the heavens. The wind lifted the wings of night. Underneath her she felt the earth, galloping.

The next day they took the horses into the hills. They followed a trail that hugs the river. It was a cold summer day and white clouds billowed mountainously above them. They waded across a tributary stream. Above it, on a hill, they found a small, abandoned shack, a collapsed outhouse, two broken-down corrals, and in the ashes of a huge fire pit, the head of a weathered ax. Down below, near the stream again, the bleached skeletons of two horses, the rib cages collapsed like fish bones, the withers like masts in the sails of bones, the eyeholes of the skulls.

"Jack-Mormon boy lived here for a while," said her grandfather. "By himself, mostly. Said he was related to the original ranchers. Planned to rebuild it all."

As they rode toward the old ranch, she told herself that he would not answer her if she asked him what happened to the boy. He could not have been a boy, really, but a young man who came out here by himself to rebuild a dream and left a tiny, rotted shack, the remains of a fire, and the skeletons of horses. Her grandfather did not have an outhouse. He went outside, and she did now, too.

"What's a Jack-Mormon?"

"One who left the Church," he said.

"What happened?" she said.

"When?"

"To the boy."

"He got in trouble," the old man said.

They came down a steep grade and Joe told her to keep her heels down and her weight back. Better that the horse slide on its butt than go head over heels. At the bottom he asked her if she was ready to run.

"We'll run up this hill, then rest them," he said.

When they took off, she felt like nothing. She felt the mare pulse through her as the hill disappeared and opened up to sky. She pushed down on the huge body that had been waiting to go and flew so easily.

She felt like an animal.

She felt like the wind.

They looked down at the old ghost ranch, then rode in, dismounting and tying the horses to what was left of a corral, then walked amid the remnants of life. A big kitchen with an old, doorless icebox, a corner from where a huge woodstove had been removed. The stovepipe lay broken and scattered, the imprint of big stove feet carved into the wood floor like horse hooves in mud. A dusty counter where food was once passed into the eating area. They ate together. There were three sleeping buildings. One small one was filled with a collapsed iron bed frame. The other two buildings were long and narrow, some of the wooden frames of the bunks still clinging to the walls: "One for the ranch hands and older boys," her grandfather told her; "one for the children and wives."

"Why didn't they have places for each family?" she asked.

"There was only one family, darlin'," said her grandfather.

"Darlin'?" she said.

"I'm sorry," said her grandfather. "I wasn't really talking to you."

She did not understand, exactly, how it was only one family, but she understood where and when his mind got lost. She liked that he called her "darlin'." The way it rolled from his throat, fresh, loving, and low, like the sound the stallion made.

In the barn there were still the remnants of bridles hung on wall hooks, and the wooden shells of old saddles on the paddock fences.

"They left things," she said.

"Sometimes you have to leave things," he said to her.

"I want to see Grandma's grave," she said.

"Your grandmother's grave?"

"Yes."

Joe looked out a window to the empty corrals. To him, sometimes, everything seemed on the edge of ruin, but despite that, he thought, we must vow to save all of it. That was not something you told a child, that the tribute to this land, this wilderness, was that nothing human lasted, and that every life was still in the wind.

She stood next to him now and looked out the window, too.

"Do you want to die out here?" she said.

"No," he said, "I want to live here. Like everybody else who's come here, your grandma included."

"What about that boy?" she said to him. "What about that boy who lived in the shack?"

He touched Elena on her shoulder. He had yet to hug her in these few days, and now he took her in his arms. She came to him without resistance, still enough of a child to have nothing in her nerves, her muscles, her bones, but trust and simplicity. He tousled her hair.

"Have you lost any friends?" he said.

"A girl in our school died in a car accident. A boy at a bus stop. A gang shot him."

"Was he in another gang?"

Elena shrugged. This was her world. Children shot each other. Whether on purpose or by accident, it mattered little.

"Dad killed two boys," she said, "who tried to steal Mom's car."

He knew that. Two boys had stopped her mother, his daughter, at a stoplight in the San Fernando Valley. She'd been taking the car to get serviced and the girl's father had been following in his truck. The boys had guns and pulled her mother from the car. They did not see her father, who, while a hundred people watched in fear from their cars, ran the boys down.

"I know," he said. "They would have killed your mother."

"Dad got in a lot of trouble anyway," she said.

"Yes, I know."

Outside the sky thickened in the northwest and the air smelled like rain. They mounted and headed back at a canter, and then a run as the clouds broke open, the air wet, dark, glorious, the horses full with heat and the wind like swirling ghosts.

"Tell me about the boy," she said to her grandfather. "You can tell me. I know about things."

"People come out here to get away," said Joe, getting up and taking the supper plates to the water pump in the sink. He primed the pump, then rinsed the dishes in the cold water that gushed from the scoop spout. Thunder rolled over the cabin and the red horses moved under the aluminum roof in the corner of their corral. "People want to get away for lots of reasons."

"Did he want to keep women like at the ranch?"

"They were polygamists out there," he said. He went to the cupboard and for the first time showed her the brown bottle. It had a turkey on the label and was topped with a cork. "Those women made choices.

All of them, men and women, came out here to be left alone."

"Like you. And Grandma."

"Sort of."

He had one shot glass. He put a smidgen in and pushed it toward her. "Just touch your lip to it," he said, "then lick it."

"I know what it is," she said.

"Like anything, it's something that can help or hurt."

She kissed the liquid, then ran her tongue over the smooth lip of the shot glass. It burned her and she shuddered slightly, but she liked the way it made her push air through her nose in bursts, like a bull.

"You feel big now?" her grandfather said.

"Mom says those women don't really have a choice," Elena said.

"Maybe," he said. Choice was a tough one. What was a real choice? It had been years since he thought about it. Not since his wife. He'd been happy enough out here, as happy as he could be without her, having every moment of survival forced upon him, happy not having choices to make.

"Why did they go?"

"They were found out, I suppose. They moved on. That's how they do it."

But he knew more than that. "My father always does this to me," she said. "He thinks it's all so complicated. So evil. That it can't be explained to a child. But I'm not a child anymore."

"You're a child a lot longer than you ever think," he said to her.

The sun was deep down under the mountains now and the rain beat hard on the roof. The light from the lantern was the only light in the world.

"What if it happened to me?" she said to him. "What if some man did something to me?"

"What!" he said. He said it abruptly. He felt his anger surge up from someplace unrecognizable. He did not want to end up with her where her parents had ended up, unable to speak to her about anything important. That's why she was here. He'd thought, at first, that they would bond over the unspeakable, but he realized now, suddenly, that he'd made no plans to talk to her at all. He'd thought he would wordlessly teach, then move on, back to his own silence. But here was a child, a young woman, a child, who was opening herself up to everything, who wanted everything without knowing what any of it was. That was the point, of course, that you could not escape up here, and it wasn't because you couldn't run from yourself, but that you simply couldn't run, you couldn't run at all.

Elena winced when she saw his anger, because she did not want to make him into her father, but she needed him to help her run, run headlong, wild, not from anything, but into everything. Could he see that?

"All right," he said. He poured himself whiskey and drank down a full shot. She took the glass and he poured her another thimble, which she licked this time with her tongue.

"One night," he said, "a girl showed up here at the ranch. It was raining, like tonight, and late. Your grandma was alive then; the girl woke us up. She was barefoot and had blood on her stomach and chest. Not her blood. Someone else's."

Elena picked up the glass and licked at the whiskey once, twice.

"Her feet were pretty cut up, too," he said, "from running in the chaparral. She said she'd come here, to the Winds, that's what they call this area, the

Wind River, with a friend, and the girlfriend of that boy who was trying to rebuild the ranch. She said they were supposed to spend the weekend riding, but when they got there the horses were dead. They'd been hobbled, you know, staked with their legs tied, by the stream. The boy told them that the week before there'd been a big storm. The stream flooded and the hobbled horses drowned. You saw the skeletons today."

"Was there a storm?"

"Yes."

"How could he leave his horses?"

"It scared the girls, too. They asked the boy to take them home, but he refused, and when they tried to leave on their own they found that he'd hidden the raft that he'd used to bring them across the river. Then, that night when they were asleep, he burned their shoes."

"He hurt them," she said.

"He forced himself on them. You understand what I'm saying."

"It's in the news all the time," said Elena.

"No," he said, "not really. That's what your father tries to say. It is complicated and evil."

"It doesn't seem complicated," she said.

"The girl kept a knife that she hid under her sleeping bag. When he came to her the next night, she stabbed him."

Elena had finished her whiskey and her grandfather took the glass back, filled it, then drained it.

She took the glass. "I'd like a little more," she said.

"Only a little more, and when I'm done," he told her.

Elena grabbed the bottle and smelled the top. "You smell like this sometimes," she said.

"Sometimes," he said. Gently, he took the bottle back. "She said that the boy hit his girlfriend and the other girl, then went outside and locked them inside the shack. He started a big bonfire. That's where we saw the ax head today. While he was out there the girl broke open the back window, crawled out, and ran here. She was lucky, you know. Brave and lucky. She didn't know there was anyone else out here. She couldn't have crossed the river to the road. She could have gone in any number of hopeless directions.

"We got her warm and dry and bandaged her feet, then your grandma and me got the guns and saddled up and rode over there."

"Grandma, too?"

"If it wasn't for me your grandma would have killed him. When we got there that kid's eyes were round and crazy. He was still out there at the fire. He denied everything, but your grandma put the rifle on him and I found the other women in the shack. The girl's friend, she came back with us, but his girlfriend stayed there with him. She wouldn't leave him."

"He was wounded," Elena said.

"Yes."

"She made a choice," she whispered.

"Maybe," he said. "I don't know. I don't know exactly what the choice was."

"Why don't you?" she insisted. "Why don't you know?"

"We got back here and we called the authorities," her grandfather said, "but by the time they got out here, the boy and his girlfriend had cleared out."

"Did the police catch him?"

"They came here and lectured the two girls. They told them they should have known better."

"Should have known what?"

Joe drank straight from the bottle. "I told you it's complicated," he whispered sadly.

"I don't understand," she said. "You've scared me and I don't understand!"

"When your father saved your mother from those boys, they arrested him. He spent time in jail. He was tried for manslaughter. He got off, but they tried him!" he said to the girl.

But suddenly she did not want to listen and she could not understand anything. She was little when her father did those things and she'd thought he'd just gone away for a while. She didn't know he went on trial or spent time in jail. Why didn't she know? And she couldn't understand whether the woman in her grandfather's story was stupid or brave, or whether anything bad had really happened to her at all.

"What about Grandma?" she said. She pushed the shot glass at him.

But he corked the bottle. "Another night," he said.

"I want more. And I want to know. I want to know everything!"

He uncorked the bottle and gave her a tiny bit, because he did not want it to be special, did not want it to be something else she could be refused. And she took it down, painfully.

"After it rains the horses come," he said. "I don't know why, but they come."

"Can we ride with them?"

"Yes," he said. It felt so good for him to tell her yes.

Later in the night she heard him walking and she got up from her sleep to find him outside staring at the sky, watching the clouds break up, as if the thick-edged storm could not hold itself together under the simple, deadly light of summer stars.

She did not disturb him. She went to the stallion, whose answers flung from his breath and his hooves, and whose eyes imagined her freedom.

A waning crescent moon came up behind the gray cliffs and the old man
stood under the Wyoming sky thinking
that his granddaughter was inside,
asleep. She looked so much like his wife.

He counted the days till the new moon. He
thought of the dark moon catching the sun in the center of the summer sky where, in the darkness, winter
stars shined. All light is backward and then, like everything, it passes and the day returns.

What was the age of the world? What was time
but the measure of lives, of children, of real women
and real men? You fill your life and then watch it
empty. And then you dip down to fill it again.

Before dawn he went to the barn to bring the stallion in, because if the wild horses came he did not want the animal outside in the corral where everything, sound, smell, sight, would call. He found Elena asleep in a corner of the paddock, her head on her knees.

The yellow stallion stood over her.

The horse lowered his head.

The girl's hair moved under his breath.

Joe went back outside. Pegasus, who rose before midnight, stood at the top of the sky. The old man knew he could not stop what would come any more then he could stop the flying horse from crossing the heavens. He walked to the back of the barn and closed the doors behind the stallion's paddock, then went back in and woke Elena.

Joe got Elena from the corral and they saddled two sorrel mares.

"Listen," he said as the sun broke in the saddle of two peaks to the east. "Listen."

And in the distance, as if she could hear them on the other side of the world, came the murmur of their thundering.

"They're still a long way off," he said.

"Will there be a stallion?"

"We're no threat on these mares. The herd will run."

They packed water, hardtack, and jerky. He attached a rope to each saddle. "If you stay I'll teach you how to rope," he said.

"I want to stay," she whispered.

He gave her a knife with a black handle and a notch where her thumb could flip the blade out with a flick. She had to press another lever to unlock it and fold the blade back in. "You can keep that," he said.

She mounted. She felt as if the sunlight itself were running. The earth smelled wet and the wind was full of expectation.

"The mares run the show," Joe said. "Anybody who knows horses knows that. Stallions just fight and follow."

"But they're beautiful," she said.

"Start at a walk. We'll do plenty of running," he told her.

As they rode the mares over the chaparral, she dreamed. Over one rise, then another, past the gully where he'd shown her how to fire the rifle. She dreamed. The Wyoming prairie infinitely fell and rose. And she dreamed she was a stallion.

"They don't just follow," she said to her grandfather.

"No," he said, "they don't."

She dreamed that if she could not be a stallion, then she would be married to one, not a man, not a metaphor as her father would insist, but the horse itself, and not as a mare, but as a woman. A marriage of freedom and beauty and flight. And as she rode his neck she would feel the rumble roll through his throat and withers. They would raise their heads to the same sweet air. See with the same eyes. Sweat the same hot sweat. She could dream this simple dream that would never go away, but go deeper and deeper inside her until it became the untouchable wild, the irrepressible wild. Her grandmother. Her mother. This dream.

In the middle of the hot day they stopped to eat. They had been riding a long time.

"I thought we heard them," she said.

"We did."

"But I can't hear them now."

"Sound travels at night," he said. "Besides, they move."

He passed her the canteen and she drank long.

"Not too much. Like in the movies, not too much."

"I wish I had a beer," she told him.

"You're not really thirsty if you want a beer," he said.

She gave him back the canteen. "Drink as much as you want," she said and could not hold back her laugh. He laughed, too. Then she touched his arm, gently. She did not even know why. "Grandpa," she said.

"What?"

"That's all," she said to him. "I just wanted to say that."

"We're going to go through a pass and go up a bit, then come to a meadow with a stream," he said.

"Yes?"

He said, "I have a feeling they'll be there."

They mounted and rode out. They came over a rise, then down again where a canyon opened up, the rocks slightly red. Above them, in the summer sky, she knew what was behind the sun. The dogs, the twins, the lynx. She drew a line straight from the top of the sky, through her heart, to the other side of the earth and the heavens below. He was waiting down there. She knew that you did not have to see something to know it. That you could feel the earth shaking for you when no one else felt anything at all.

Something made the wind move. Would it matter if it were the wings of a horse? Something made the sky break open and roll with sound. What would change if it were really his running?

The canyon broke into a meadow, flat and green with grass. A stream crawled through. The mountains surrounded them suddenly like a crown.

"They're not here," Elena said.

"Listen."

She heard the wind on the sagebrush. She thought she could hear the water in the stream. Then her horse raised its head, its nostrils flexing.

Joe turned to her. "Can you hear them?" he said. "Now?"

Their rumble echoed from the opposite canyon and into the meadow. More than even hearing, she could feel them.

"They come through here on their way to a plateau on the other side there," her grandfather said. He pointed beyond the stream. "There's a small lake up there, a watering hole, where they drink, then they feed their way back down."

"We saw them come by your ranch," she said.

"Sometimes they do. Not often. Did you want to wait and see?" He pointed again. "They'll come busting out of that canyon mouth. They'll swerve when they see us. Sit tight. Let 'em get by, then we'll run for the back of the herd."

Her grandfather breathed heavily with expectation. Even he, who had seen the horses a hundred times and run with them, sweated with anticipation at the thunder of their approach. The mares quivered in the charged air.

He touched her shoulder. "Just ride her, darlin'. She'll head right in. When we hit the plateau, they'll start to pull up and we'll just veer out. Just ride her."

He watched her closely. She thought at that moment that she was not ready, that she did not ride well enough, that this was not the thing for a young girl to do, because suddenly that is how she felt, small and young. He watched the sweat form on her temple and trickle down beside her ear.

"Are you afraid?" he said.

But she could hear the horses coming. She could feel them now inside her. And when they broke into the meadow, fanning out in their dark, pounding fury, her own horse pulled up. She pulled the reins steadily down to her knee, shifting her weight, and circled the animal back again to face the herd, which had veered away at the sight of them, as her grandfather had said. Already Joe had struck out after them with his horse. When he turned back for her, his animal reared its head to the fury of the herd and he could barely pull her up enough before Elena struck out, too, her mare surging at the massive, single body that moved across the meadow.

In seconds they were with them, and then within them. Running. They flew across the flat plain and up into the canyon. Elena saw her grandfather slapping at his horse with his reins as he ran outside the herd, but she took her own horse in, the bodies of the animals around her surging forward. But for the movement of the horse, space disappeared in the timeless running of the herd, the eternal running that the land had known for thousands of years, before humans came, before the horses disappeared, and then the Spanish came and the horses returned to lay their feet in the same soft earth. There on the horse, with the wild horses, she rode, without awareness, in the history of timeless everything.

They soon came to the end of the canyon and the opening of the plateau. The herd slowed and spread to the water and she pulled her horse from the pack, circling. Her grandfather met her. Her horse, snorting hard, sweating, the heavy stink of exertion everywhere around them.

The stallion, a medium-size paint, raised up and came around the back of the herd, running the perimeter, head raised, watching the man and the girl saddled on their mares and gulping at the thin mountain air.

The old man squinted under his hat and it was difficult for the girl to interpret the tears that ran from the corners of his eyes, but she could not deny the swell in her own heart as she broke down, sobbing. His horse was next to hers and he put his arm around her. He wept for the past and memory. And the girl cried.

The sun was glorious. Somewhere, something

flew amid the invisible stars. A murmur rose from the settling herd and the stallion returned to the water hole to drink. The girl wiped her eyes. Her chest throbbed. All she could feel was longing.

They walked their horses back to the meadow. This time she noticed the budding sage, the wildflowers yellow and blue across the hills, orange, lavender, and white over the purple-headed chaparral.

"The Comanche are from here," Joe said.

"I thought Texas," she answered. She knew a little about them, that they were nomadic, that they fought the cavalry, that they rode.

"Their roots are Shoshone. They migrated down to Texas and pushed the Apache out in the late sixteen hundreds."

"Grandma was part Comanche," Elena said.

"Yes," he said. "And so's your mom. And so are you."

Why didn't she ever think of it? She'd been told she was Indian. Part Indian. Some small part. But she'd just been told and had never asked more.

"When a Comanche child was born she was taken by her mother to her horse, then to the father. When a horse was born, it bonded first to its mother, and then to the child who would ride it. They trained the horse for riding in its first hour of life, imprinted it and bonded it to its rider. They were the best riders in the world. Even better than the Mexicans."

"Mexicans are Indian, too," she said.

"A lot of them," he said. "The Comanche lived with their horses. Horses were equals. Family."

"You're explaining to me about Grandma."

"Yes," he said, "and to myself, about you."

"Are we going to Grandma's grave now?" she asked him.

"Darlin'," he said softly, "we were already there."

That evening when they got back the dogs had flushed out a flock of range chickens and Joe shot one with the scoped .22. Elena helped him pluck and gut it, and they ate it with new potatoes that night. It was a cold, clear night and Joe brought the dogs in to sit by the stove and chew bones. The cat moved around them, waiting. Her grandfather got out the whiskey and the two of them had a small toast.

"To wild horses," he said.

And she said, "To wild horses." The whiskey was hot with her pride.

"Have you already smoked pot?" he asked her.

"Yes," she said.

"What else?"

"That's all. Some kids do acid."

"Acid," he said, nodding slightly.

"Mom and Dad did it, you know, back in the hippie days."

"They did?" he said.

"Yes, you know that," she said. "But they don't want me to."

"Of course not." He laughed. "Well, I don't have any pot here."

"Indians smoked things," she said.

"I'm sure they did," he answered. He did not want to know any more, or to argue. He'd just wanted to test her honesty, and she'd been unabashed.

She herself did not feel she had anything to hide.

"Anyways, it's expensive," Elena said.

Joe got up and went to a chest near the wall and got out a woven blanket and put it around the girl's shoulders. He did not have to tell her it was her grandmother's. She knew.

"Do you remember when your grandmother and I came out here?" he said to her.

"I was really little," she said.

"Your grandmother was younger than me. And healthier. I was supposed to die, not her."

"Mom always says that to Dad."

"I'll bet," he said. "When rodeo started back in the beginning of the century there were events for women, but that ended in the thirties. I don't know why. After that the only thing they let women do was race barrels, which is what your grandma did."

"Now women have their own rodeo," said Elena.

"Now," he said, "but not then. Barrel racing's still the only thing for women in the big game. For a few years, your grandma was the best. When she quit riding she made a lot of money as a trainer, then as a trader and breeder, then she quit that, too, and we sold everything and bought this land out here. For the longest time we just kept the horses over here and lived in a trailer back across the river where I keep the pickup truck now. There's a flatboat that comes down here if you make arrangements back in Pinedale. That's how we got the heavy stuff across, and still do. Your mom worried about us out here."

"Yes," she said.

"I got that in common with your father," Joe said. "We met women who changed our lives and made more money than we did in the end."

"I know why you live here," she said.

"Yes," he said, "but you see, you don't get away from anything. One neighbor is a bad neighbor."

"You don't have neighbors now."

"People come through. Something always happens. I think we came out here thinking we could stop everything from happening."

He gave Elena a little more whiskey. "I don't want to try to tell you that you can't hold on to anything. Because," he said, "because you have to try to hold on to everything anyway."

She did not understand that, and he could see that she did not understand.

"I just want to ride rodeo," Elena said.

"All right," he said. "Good." He drank some himself. "That stallion out there is not the one she rode in rodeo. It's his son. Your grandma trained him."

"Why don't you ride him?"

"We weren't out here too long when your grandma got cancer," he said.

"I knew she had cancer," said the girl. "You came to L.A. the last time I saw her, and you. I was six."

"We fought with your mother," he said.

"I know."

"Had I known what your grandma was up to, I'd have fought her, too."

"Mom wanted you to stay in Los Angeles."

"We said good-bye. Your grandma promised to come back and go in the hospital if she got worse. We took a trip to Mexico, then came back here."

"But she got worse right away?" Elena said.

Her grandfather got up. The dogs raised their heads and the cat moved in, snatching a bone and heading under a bunk. A coyote pack yelped wildly, then quieted. It got quiet enough that the girl could hear the mares snorting in their corral.

"A kill," Joe said.

She told herself she would remember that sound, so different from the usual lonely howling across the hills. The piling up of yelp upon yelp, as if the killers themselves had lost something deep and important to them, not brought it down.

"I loved her so much," said her grandfather. "I loved her so much."

And watching him cry she felt something that she had never before felt, and even in feeling it, lost it and longed for feeling it again. She came inside his life and saw him young. She felt her insides torn. She opened the door to her parents' bedroom and saw her father clinging to her mother in an embrace deeper than love, deeper than understanding, illicitly deep and transient, his fingers white like bones. She saw the eternity of pain in the liquid of her mother's eyes when she said, Elena, I love you, Elena. She thought she would never love without feeling the longing she felt right then.

"Old men cry too much," said her grandfather. He sat back down. "We came back. We rode together over the hills. No one could ride like her." He looked at the girl wrapped in her grandmother's blanket and who knew what he was thinking, though he had not brought her here to ride like her grandmother, to ride in the fire of her grandmother's wind.

"I ride like her," Elena said.

"That night," he said, "your grandmother came to me in our bed and said, 'This is how you will remember me.' In the morning she and the stallion were gone.

"At first I thought she'd just gone out for a ride, but by afternoon I was thinking about what she'd said and I saddled up a mare and headed after her. I don't track that well, but up over that first ridge I could see she'd let that horse fly, and soon, after an hour anyway, those tracks still showed that she was galloping and I figured out that even following at a canter, as late as I'd started, I was falling farther off her pace every minute out."

"She had to stop sometime," said Elena.

"You don't know that horse, or your grand-mother. I came back and packed an extra horse with gear and went back on her trail. Your grandma hadn't taken anything. Just the horse, and now she'd been out over a day. It was pretty clear what she'd done. I lost her trail by nightfall. It took me a week to find that meadow and lake."

"Was grandma still alive when you found her?" the girl whispered.

"I found the horse leading that herd, his bridle and saddle gone. I never found your grandma."

"She set him free," Elena said.

"Herself, too," he said. "She was gonna die anyway."

It was quiet. She heard the dreaming of the dogs and the horses muttering.

"But she's not dead," said Elena. "She's missing."

"I brought that horse back," said Joe. "It took me a year to catch him. I knew everything that herd did, everywhere they went. But I brought him back. And I never rode him."

"What's his name?" Elena said.

"He's too much animal for a name," said her grandfather.

But she realized then that none of his animals had names, and she told him.

"Ah," he said, "they can name themselves."

They both laughed. For the first time she perceived him as funny and peculiar. She admired that he lived his life in his own special way. She reached for the bottle and poured her own whiskey. "Grandma drank whiskey?"

"Yes," he said. "Regulate yourself."

"I'll ride it," she said proudly. "It won't ride me." She touched it to her lips, feeling what her grandmother felt, the same brown burn under the same stars, the same wind, the same stallion outside who could, at any time, she knew it now, leap the fence and head back into the wild, though he had not. "Mom and Dad think you buried Grandma out here somewhere."

"Better that," he said.

"Now you ride with the herd," she said.

But he did not answer.

"When you ride with the herd you visit Grandma," said Elena. "She loved you so much, Grandpa." Because she did not understand jealousy or death, only immortality and beauty. In her innocence she saw him more truly than he saw himself.

58

That night Elena could not sleep. She waited for her grandfather's slumbering breaths, then went to the barn.

The yellow stallion came to her as softly as memory. So she saddled him. She chose the lightest bit, because she knew she would not need to control him with a heavy hand. She tacked him, opened the corral, and led him out. Then she placed the reins over his head.

His breath steamed the cold air and when she took his mane she felt him shaking. She put her foot in the stirrup and was upon him.

And to him, her weight was nothing but the answer to some distant longing. A moment under the saddle, and then the pressure of her legs, the unburdening. The air smelled so sweetly of night and moon, the sliver of crescent moon that they joined on the hill. She moved. He turned. And they were gone.

They flew across the setting moon. There, in the predawn, on the divide between the darkness and the light, they chased the winged horse across the sky.

Her grandfather did not awaken, even as he heard the horse hammering the air, climbing the mountain, taking off into the heavens. He dreamed them flying. He saw that time went backward and forward, back and forth, and after the dream of Elena's riding he spent the infinite night deep in his lover's arms. He awoke like a man who had made love all night, to a morning that begged for him. He went to the barn to wait for their return. To wait for the girl and the stallion.

Joe started her out roping barrels from about five feet away. He'd known plenty of men who struggled with roping because the movement was so different from throwing—a crossing movement, not a downward one—the wrist flicking flat and in, the opposite from throwing a football or baseball or serving with a tennis racket. She had the advantage, she told him, of having no good habits.

"That's what your mother would say," he answered. "My advantage is that I'm old and ignorant." Which is what he wanted to believe, that he would simply grow older and more open to everything.

They backed away to ten feet, changed to roping a plastic steer head, which he stuck to the end of a hay bale with two long metal prongs. By the end of the morning she roped the barrels and steer head from horseback, standing still.

"The mares are too slow and safe," said Elena.

"They're fast enough," he said. "A safe horse is a stubborn horse. You get overconfident you'll get bucked off in a blink."

She laughed and he wondered what she remembered. When he'd seen her six, seven years ago, she'd seemed a timid child. But back then everything was in such crisis.

In the afternoon he set out the barrels in a big triangle, each barrel twenty yards apart, and let her saddle the stallion. She took him around at a walk, a slow trot, a fast trot, and finally a slow canter. The stallion took to the barrels as if he had never forgotten. The girl took to the stallion as if memory preceded birth. By the next day she rode the circuit at a gallop, completing a run around the barrels in twenty-five seconds.

"How fast for the rodeo?" Elena asked her grandfather.

"Depends on the level," he said. "And the size of the ring. A ring this size, seventeen, eighteen seconds might win a high school or college rodeo. You'd have to come in under fifteen for pro."

"I'm not that far off."

"You're a long way off."

"Just ten seconds."

"In barrel racin' a tenth of a second is an eternity. The closer you get to fifteen seconds, the farther you are away."

He said those kinds of things, she knew. He liked those kinds of mysteries, which were only so true, or true enough, or true for some. But for her, on this yellow horse, problems were tiny things, things to roll over like thunder and crack open like lightning.

* * *

Before Elena came to the Winds, he'd grazed the mares by rotating them, letting two out to feed and keeping two in, one for reserve and one for riding out to gather up the others. This was as long as the herd was not close by. Now he let three mares run and took the girl out on the stallion to round them up, teaching her to herd from behind, pushing the animals forward and right or left by riding the haunch.

By the end of the week she shot her first rabbit, gutted and skinned it with her own knife. Now she understood the sense of the hunt, of taking life for life, of taking only what she needed. Elena found gratification in its intensity, in knowing what she had taken and how she had taken it, and compared it to the blindness of eating animals bred for slaughter.

At the end of the second week she knew her parents were coming, and on a ride back from rounding up the mares she asked him to let her stay.

"You can't stay," he said. "You have a life."

"Just longer," she said. "Just long enough to get better."

Joe watched his granddaughter, whom he loved. Now he would be lonely again. He'd thought that he'd been lonely and that he was done with it, that he was already as lonely as he could possibly be, and he would live till death in that comfortable loneliness. Now he saw that he could yet be more lonely.

Both parents got on the phone when he called them.

"She's missing ballet," said Elena's mother, Calamity Ray.

"Two more weeks," the old man said.

"She's supposed to test for her black belt," her father, Harlan, said.

"When we first talked, you didn't even want her," said Calamity Ray.

"Well, she's more capable than I thought," he told her. "We're having fun."

"That's important," said the father.

"Has it snowed?" said Calamity Ray. "Every time I come to Wyoming it snows."

"Well, wait two more weeks," said Joe. "We don't need snow."

"We're coming out. We'll talk about it there," said her mother.

He hung up the phone. He told Elena, "They're coming."

"Black belt?" he said to her.

During the phone call she'd sat on the floor, oiling her saddle.

"The early belts don't mean much," Elena said. "It's all the black belt and the degrees after." She looked up at him and smiled. "There's an eternity between each degree," she said.

"Is that so?"

"You know," she said, "the higher you get, the farther you are away."

"So I've heard."

They laughed together. He always underestimated her. Or overestimated her. He'd forgotten. She understood discipline and accomplishment. And she could be a child in one minute and wise in the next.

"Were you always a cowboy?" she asked.

"I was never a cowboy," he said.

"You are now."

"No," he said.

"Did you fight in your war?"

"Yes," he said. He moved the lantern closer to her and sat down.

"Dad didn't like the war he fought in."

"Nobody likes the war they fight in."

"It's not that. You know what I'm saying." She didn't like it when he was difficult like this and she had to fight him for everything. She liked him when he told her stories about who he was, who her grandmother was. And when he made silly contradictions sound like truth. "He said if he had it to do over he wouldn't go. Lots of his friends didn't go."

"But he doesn't have it to do over," Joe said.

She worked the oil into the saddle. She liked the feel and smell of the leather, the buttery-soft texture, the sweetness. It made her think of riding, and of being ridden. It was that, the thought of the steel bit in her own mouth, that gave her such a light touch, that let her guide her stallion with her body and her thighs.

"So when did you become a cowboy?"

"You just want me to talk about your grandmother," he said. "You know it hurts me a little to talk about her."

"Yes," she said.

But it did not matter that it hurt. It simply hurt. She knew this and he knew it, too.

"I was born in Southern California," he said, "but my parents moved back to Philadelphia and sold cars. I left college to fight in Korea."

"I know about that war," she said. "I had a history teacher who fought in it. He said it was so cold they had to pee on their rifles to make them work."

"I never peed on my rifle," said her grandfather. That was the problem with talking about war.

The horror did not translate. He touched her cheek. "I hope you never have to face evil," he said.

"Then you met Grandma," she said, pressing him.

"When I got out of the service I took a job with Texaco and got sent out to Oklahoma City. I met your grandma at a dance bar. We started courting and she taught me to ride then. She always could ride. She was brought up with it. Her family still had a little land left from when the government divided up the Comancheria for the last time. They had horses there. But back then, that was her parents' heritage, not hers. She was trying to leave all that."

"She was pretty."

"Of course she was. She had an olive color to her skin like your mom. It turned reddish brown in the sun, and her hair bleached out light, like yours. You have her dark eyebrows, too. She was a reporter then. She could take pictures if she had to. Real smart. But when she got something in her head you couldn't change it."

"Like me."

"Yes, like most people, I guess, but most people don't turn it into anything positive. I loved to see her in a dress. Your mother's line; you have great legs. But your grandmother liked pants and boots."

"Like Mom."

"We got married. She had two miscarriages before she had your mom. You know what that is?"

"Mom had one before me."

"Well," he said. "Really." She'd never told him that. Of course, he'd fought her, her generation, with its loose sex and abortions, along with everything else. He'd said then that they'd pay. Now he didn't believe in paying. Not paying for. Not paying back.

"She worked a few years before she noticed

that men hired after her, young kids, were passing her for raises and promotions. Then after she had your mom—she had to leave work, you know; they didn't have day care back in the fifties—they wouldn't let her back to work at the paper at all.

"That's when she got back on a horse. She said she was going to do something that had to be measured by the clock. No judging involved. No one could argue with the clock."

"No men in barrel racing either," said the girl.

"Well," he said, "I guess that's true. Not that it would have mattered. I don't think a man could run those barrels as fast as your grandmother anyway."

"So?"

"So that's it. That's all. She was the best. Texaco started moving me around the country, though it didn't matter much because your grandmother had to move around for all the rodeos. Your mother hated it, you know that, all that moving, never having roots or friends."

"She travels a lot now for her books."

"Well, life's ironic," he said. His daughter, who rejected her traveling parents, her cowgirl mother, now the itinerant cowgirl poet. "When Grandma retired from barrel racing she started training quarter horses, then got enough money to buy a ranch and start breeding them. Texaco tried to transfer me to Saudi Arabia and when I said no, that's when my promotions and raises stopped coming. I got early retirement."

But she did not understand. They still had a ranch. Horses. Her own mother abandoned that dream life to teach college in Los Angeles, to live in a sprawling, urban war zone. Her grandparents left it to come here. She knew nothing about the lives of these people, her own family, and was so hungry now for everything: what they did, who they were, but the more she was told, the less she understood. And if this were not a labyrinth enough, she wondered now about her father, his family, his history.

She suddenly, inexplicably, felt worse than she had ever felt, worse than before she came here hating everyone and everything. She did not even realize until now that that was what she had felt. Hate. And now, without hate, she had nothing.

She saw the lives of everyone around her laid bare, strip-mined. Ugly, ordinary, sympathetic. She began to cry.

She just wanted to know who she was. That was simple enough. And she wanted to know about her grandmother, who had already lived and died. A complete, unknowable life, already here, and then, like smoke, already gone.

"I need more," she said. "There has to be more. I need to know more."

Joe looked at his granddaughter and saw a sensitive, beautiful child. "We all, always, need more," he said, and immediately he felt foolish. "You wanted a better story?" he said softly, and felt more foolish still.

"Why did you come here?" she cried.

"How can you say that?" he answered her. "How can you sit here and say that?"

"Because I am here!" She screamed at him. "You lived lives and then just came out here to die! Then what? Then what!" But as her voice echoed in her own mind, she felt the haunting intimation that in the echo she had already been answered.

The next night after riding, Elena showered behind the cabin, using rainwater that they'd saved and warmed in a plastic bag hung from the roof and exposed to the southern sun. In the morning she put on clean clothes. Her parents called from Pinedale, saying they'd arrived and were heading in. Joe and Elena saddled the stallion and three mares and rode down to the river to meet them.

Elena, mounted, held the horses as her grandfather rowed across the Green River. Her parents had parked their rented sedan in the hollow under the gray cliffs, next to Joe's pickup truck. Though the day was warm and the sky yellow-blue, gray clouds hung on the snowy head of Square Top Mountain above the Winds. Her parents waved to her and she waved back. Everyone hugged on the other side, and then they came back over, her grandfather pointing the boat against the current to keep it crossing on a straight line.

Everyone always said how handsome they were, her parents, how they were so wild and strange, these people with whom she'd spent almost every day of her life and found so ordinary. She watched her mother's hair, flaxen and shoulder length, blow from underneath her straw cowgirl hat. She'd seen a picture of her, taken with her roommate during her first year of college, only a few years older than Elena was now. Her mother stood behind the roommate, a hand at her mouth, her chin tilted slightly down, her eyes looking up, huge and doelike.

She could tell her father was nervous to let Joe do all the rowing. He sat slightly forward, his arm around her mother. Her mother always called him a dreamer. A dreamer. Her father. Now she wondered what he dreamed.

They hugged her when they came ashore, but she felt the burdensome pregnancy of silence as her mother took in the yellow horse.

Calamity Ray already felt loss and defeat. If they were to ride with her mother's ghost, wouldn't it have been better if they had saddled the fourth mare as well as the stallion, and gone to the cabin with the yellow horse saddled and riderless?

"It's not snowing," said Joe.

"Not yet," said Calamity Ray.

In fact the day was as good as Wyoming had, warm with a soft breeze coming from the southwest, whispering over the chaparral.

They mounted and rode along the river, avoiding the shack built and abandoned by the Mormon boy, though they stopped at the ghost ranch, riding up to the old corral.

"Why don't you go in and show your parents some work," Joe said.

Elena didn't understand why they had not gone back to the cabin, why Joe did not take her there to work the stallion, but she saw the look in her mother's eyes, the same look she had before crying.

"She can handle that horse, I guess," said her father.

And Joe said, "She can handle any horse."

Elena took the stallion into the corral, her body forward as the horse lunged into a gallop around the pen. With a slight, backward lean she brought him to a slow trot. She turned him on a dime and broke forward again, changing leads. The huge animal, who looked as if nothing in the world could hold him, held himself to the girl.

Joe hadn't immediately taken them to the cabin where his wife's ghost rode. He'd avoided the shack of the boy pioneer who thought the wilderness had made him a god. Here, under a gentle, blue sky that whispered yes to everything, Elena flew on her powerful stallion. Calamity Ray could smell his sweat in the wind.

Elena took off again, leaping over a breach in the fence. The pounding of the animal's hooves was so much more than sound, like a heartbeat carried through the visceral air.

"My God," said the father. "Who'd have thought?"

"It's amazing, isn't it?" said Joe.

"Yes," whispered the girl's mother, while she held back a million things that she knew, once stated, would change nothing. It was the kind of whisper that held everything, the earth, the sky, the world, the stars, together with its glue. And the kind of sound that could tear everything apart. "Yes."

Joe and Calamity rode back to the cabin together while Elena rode with her father over the hill.

"You don't ride so bad," Joe said to his daughter.

"I've been taking lessons," she said. "Some of my appearances are at rodeos and horse shows. I have to ride out."

"Well, life has its twists," he said.

"The ironies are perfectly clear to me," said Calamity Ray.

They rode in silence for a little while before he spoke again. "She wants to ride rodeo," Joe said.

"They don't do rodeo at Harvard or Stanford," said Calamity Ray.

"Cornell?" he said.

"Polo and equitation. You know that. She'd have to go to some farm campus in the West."

"They give degrees, don't they?" said Joe.

"I'm sure you know the difference between Yale and Aggie Tech," she said. "One opens doors, one shuts them. What will she have after rodeo? After she breaks all her bones?"

"Her own life to live," he said.

She did not need to remind him that he was the same father who pulled her out of art school to get a "real" degree from the University of Virginia, "something she could fall back on." Those were his precise words.

"Well, it's a long way off," he said.

"Nothing is a long way off," she answered.

For a while they rode in silence again, his cabin coming into view as they topped the next ridge.

"I want that child to have everything," the daughter whispered.

"She might be better off without it."

Now furious, she turned on him with the same quick temper his granddaughter had flung at him only two nights before.

"Stop with your meaningless banalities! Now you don't have any answers when before you did. Well, for you that's fine! That girl was almost killed on a horse. You know that!"

He saw that she was on the verge of accusing him of bringing his wife out here to die.

"You brought Elena to me," he said.

"You didn't want her."

They'd stopped on the crest with all of western Wyoming around them, the chaparral stretching to the cliffs and the river, and the snowy mountains rising at the other horizon.

"Now I want her," he said softly.

She took her mare down the slope and he followed her.

"Why don't you just come home," she said.

"Home to what? This is my home." He knew that she was right, right about all of it, but she did not know how capable he was of forgiveness now. He forgave everyone everything. He even forgave himself. He felt no need to remind his daughter that she walked in her mother's footsteps, too, and that we all cry and flail against everyone to let us become what we must inevitably become, despite our choices, our indomitable wills, despite who we thought we were or who we dreamed to be.

"I owned a horse once," Harlan said to Elena. "Do you remember?" They rode together over the ridge. Below she could see her mother and grandfather riding toward the ranch, beyond them, the cold, huge head of Square Top Mountain, and back the other way, to the north, the teeth of the black, icy Tetons.

"I shot a rabbit here," she told him, "I skinned it myself."

"Do you remember our home in the canyon?" he said. "Before the big earthquake destroyed our house and we had to move, there was a wildfire. You were five years old. I took you on the horse and tried to ride out the back way, but we got trapped in a cave. You took a cat with you, Garbo, do you remember?"

"Mom was away," Elena said.

"That was her first big book tour."

"The cat died," she said. "From smoke."

"The horse, too," he said. "After we got out."

They rode down the hill, picking their way through the sage, then started up the next ridge. "In the foothills here," she said, "there's a mountain pasture and a lake. Me and Grandpa ride with the wild horses there."

"I rode some rodeo for a while," he said. "Do you remember that? Some team roping."

"You surfed, too."

"Yes."

"You used to take me out."

"Yes."

"But you stopped taking me."

"I stopped surfing."

"And stopped riding, too."

"After your accident. We moved out of the canyon. We all stopped."

She nudged her stallion into a trot and circled her father, who held up as she came around in front of his mare.

"We had to move because of the earthquake," she said to him. "Not because of me."

She saw him pondering his answer as if he were pouring the truth from one cup to another, measuring what he would give. It was something she hated, his sifting of what stories he would present to her until she was old enough to really understand. But he didn't have to. She remembered the horse bucking her on the trail. Her foot got caught in the cinch and the animal dragged her upside down across the rocks. Her father threw himself under the horse and shielded her from its hooves. He saved her. He was hospitalized.

"We just wanted you safe," he said.

She came around again beside him and they walked the horses.

"You killed two boys," Elena said. "Grandpa said you went to jail."

"Until I was found innocent."

"But you did kill them," she said. "And you and Mom lied. You said you just went away, but you were in jail."

"Yes," he said.

"Why did you have to kill them?"

"I didn't try to," said Harlan. "I tried to protect your mom. They had guns."

"But how did you know? How did you know that you had to kill them?"

Harlan looked at his daughter astride the golden stallion. She was new to him. She did not match the history of the self he imagined her to be. If you do not sacrifice your life, you have no life. He did not know how to tell this to his young daughter, who'd forgotten so much, wanted to know so much, who wanted to burn and burn.

"I love you, Elena," he said to her. "I'd give my life for you without thinking."

"Well, you've already thought about it then." She laughed, sounding like Calamity Ray.

But she saw that she'd hurt him and she did not mean to hurt him but simply state the truth, for a change, because truth was a hard, good thing like this land, like killing an animal with your own hands, like riding a horse. It was why, when she did not try to suppress it, she hated him. Because he thought you could just keep telling stories over and over, a different version every time, that you could live there, in that made-up world instead of here, in the one in front of you. She understood, suddenly, for a moment, that this was why her mother called him a dreamer.

"I want to ride rodeo," she said.

He said, "I'm not surprised."

"Mom will fight it."

"She's never denied you anything," said Harlan. "She let you come here."

"This is different," said the girl. "You know that."

"Can we run these horses?" Harlan said. "Do you think I can keep up with you if you let him out?"

"No," Elena said. "You can't." She gave the stallion a kick and he surged forward. In an instant her father was after her. But she put distance between them quickly, and in the widening gap he saw that he was just a man on a horse following his daughter and she, she and her horse were simply one.

But for Elena, riding out over the chaparral, the sun everywhere running, the hot life of her stallion's speed smashing at the land, the stones, the mountains, and the sky, she rode a stallion the color of the sun; he sweat beneath her. Everything was true and she was everything.

Afterward they rode back down to the river, where Joe and Harlan crossed and brought back a cooler and bags of groceries. Elena and her mother carried the groceries on their laps and the men carried the cooler between them by holding the handles. In the cooler were steaks, cold beer and sodas, some butter. The grocery bags contained sweet corn, tins of fish, salami, flour, honey, peanut butter, cooking oil, macaroni, two loaves of bread, cans of beans and cans of tomatoes, a magnum of red table wine, a bottle of expensive bourbon.

Joe fried the steaks and boiled the corn that night on the top of the woodstove. They used the butter on the corn and ate a loaf and a half of bread. They drank the wine. Calamity Ray said nothing when Joe poured out four tumblers of it and gave one to Elena. They talked about Joe's vegetable garden, her father's rabbits, the orders for her mother's forthcoming cow-girl cookbook, but they did not talk about whether or not Elena could stay another two weeks or whether she could ride rodeo.

Elena picked at her steak, meat she had not taken herself, and watched her grandfather, who ate his steak voraciously along with her parents, who themselves seldom ate meat. She felt enraged, furious at their silence and contradictions.

After dinner it was dark. Elena's parents did the dishes while Joe went out, cleaned the mares' corral and fed them. The girl went to the barn and did the same for her stallion. When she brushed his neck he put his nose on her shoulder and his soft lips pushed at her ear. She put her arm on him. She listened in his chest and heard the rumbling sound of eternity.

That night Elena dreamed that the thunder in the sky was the sound of hooves and when she went outside she saw the wild horses strung across the dome of night, the lights and the blackness swirling, the clouds swirling, the bridge of the Milky Way shuddering under the herd. And when the winged horse came by, following them, nipping at the diamond heels of the mares, he stopped for Elena. He breathed on her with his misty black breath and turned her into stars.

She awoke in the darkness and, walking out into the moonless night, found her mother and grandfather. They turned when they saw her.

"I guess sleeplessness runs in the family," said Joe.

He gave the girl's mother a hug and kissed the girl, too, before he went back inside, momentarily waking Harlan.

"I'm sorry," he said.

"It's okay," said the father, "I fall right back asleep."

"I wish I could do that," Joe said.

"You probably dream your nightmares at night," said Harlan.

"You dream yours all day?" said Joe. But the girl's father was already asleep again.

Outside Elena stood with her mother in the middle of the night. The wind whispered on the sage and the shadows sat like fat black ghosts under the starlight.

"Do you know Pegasus?" said the girl, pointing to the center of the sky.

"Yes," said her mother.

"I want to be like him," Elena said.

"He takes the same path every night," Calamity Ray said, but seeing the rage in the girl's eyes, softened. "Just an observation," she said to her. "Not a criticism."

"Wouldn't you rather ride him once and die?" said the girl.

"No," the mother said.

"Not ever? Not even when you were young?"

"Maybe," whispered her mother. "Maybe when I was young."

"You should have another child," Elena said to her mother. "You should have a baby."

"And then I'd let go of you?" her mother said. "Is that it?"

"It's not too late," said Elena.

"I want your freedom, too," Calamity Ray said to her daughter. She remembered her child so vividly she felt an ache in her breasts. She remembered how she and Elena got hungry at the same time, got ill at the same time. How she lived in the rhythm of this child, her breath, her feeding, her sleep, her dreams, the movement of her bowels. "I want it more than you do. I want you to be successful, and safe."

"You want me to be who you want me to be," said the girl.

The mares stirred, then moved in unison to the other side of the corral. When the animals quieted the mother and daughter could hear the stallion whinnying.

"Come with me," said the girl, and her mother followed her into the barn. When Elena lit a lantern, the yellow horse came inside. His back, pale and ghostlike in the shallow light, lacked only the ghost rider, the grandmother whose absence seemed more powerful than ever before. If only she were alive and in front of them now, Calamity Ray thought, weathered, old, arthritic from the broken bones of riding rodeo.

Elena went to the horse, who rumbled at her approach. He lowered his head to her arms, nuzzled her, and she buried her face in his soft nose. Then the stallion gently stepped back, breathing on the girl, his hot breath on Elena's face, her hair moving softly in his wind.

Elena turned to her mother and Calamity Ray touched her daughter's hair. She brought her daughter to her breast, where Elena rested her head uneasily.

"Let me stay," she whispered. Let me ride the horse. Let me ride.

"Of course," her mother said.

"All the money's in barrel racing," Joe said.

Elena's parents had left that morning, giving her another two weeks.

"Can I ride rodeo?" she'd asked them.

"Let's take it two weeks at a time," her father said.

For her mother, in the bargain, she had to promise to come back home and test for her black belt and stay in ballet.

"I want to do everything," Elena said to her grandfather.

"There's no money in everything. No money in women's rodeo. Just a lot of tough, tough cowgirls. Besides, that horse is a barrel racer. You'd need a good, young ranch horse for roping. I don't have calves to rope or bulls to ride and I don't have any broncos here for you to ride either."

"Let's go catch one," said the girl.

Joe didn't answer. He saddled up a mare and the girl led her stallion from his paddock to the ring. She brought out his blanket and saddle, rubbing her hands across the smooth leather. The horse nudged her but she backed away, knowing that she did not want to be too friendly with him before she asked him for a big workout. It hurt her to deny him, but even this animal would fight her, test her at the beginning of the ride, and to concede anything to him now could make him twice as stubborn later.

"Mom's making enough money now to buy a ranch," the girl said.

"Is that so?" said Joe.

"You could move in with us," said Elena.

"You know, back in college, before my war, before cars or radios or TV, the snow was deeper back then and nobody'd yet invented boots—"

"You're funny," said the girl.

"It was before your grandma. I had a crush on a sorority girl. Have you ever had a crush?" Joe said.

"Maybe," Elena said.

"Anyway, I had a little wisp of a mustache back then and the girl asked me to shave it off and I did. Then she said she liked my hair shorter and asked me to get a haircut and I did. Then she said, 'Joe, tell me you love me,' and I did. I told her I loved her. Then she dumped me. She told me I wasn't the same boy she fell in love with when we met."

"So?"

"So your mother ain't going to shave and get a haircut just for you. She's too smart."

"She doesn't have a mustache." Elena laughed.

"Well, then she won't grow one."

"She can't!"

"And she won't."

"You're just telling stories, like Dad," said Elena, mounting her horse.

"Well," said Joe, "I was a dad once, too."

She liked him when he told stories, when he was funny. Her father was once funny, she remembered. He'd made up silly songs, pretended he was afraid of clowns, took pratfalls to make her laugh. She wondered now who had changed, her or him?

"Walk him now," said her grandfather. "Let's not start out with him all revved up."

She walked the yellow stallion as her grandfather dismantled the far end of the big corral, the part away from the cabin that opened out into sage hills. Her grandmother had it built that way when she came here, to make a runway, a starting line and finishing line far enough away from the barrels.

"You're going to walk around them first," said Joe, "then trot, then a slow canter. Then you can let him out a little bit and we'll see how he takes to it. After that we'll walk him some more and settle him down before you go at it."

But from the start she had a hard time holding the animal back. It was the first time, in fact, that he did not obey her every whim.

"Walk him!" Joe yelled. "Weight back!" He knew the animal sensed the dash, the run he'd been bred for. Some horses were mad for the barrels and good for nothing else. They would almost kill their riders for that quarter minute of lightning.

The stallion broke into a trot again and the girl leaned back, jerking the reins slightly, slowing him. In the canter, twice she had to pull his head away from the turn to bring him to her.

When she finished that run her grandfather rode out to her. She was scared now for the first time. She had never been afraid of this horse. His power had always been her power, his movements hers. For the first time she felt him as an alien being, huge and willful. She thought back now, suddenly, to when her father took her surfing and she felt the immense, unimaginable power of the ocean waves. "You're nothing," her father said. "You can't fight it, you can only ride it." But this horse, this animal, had its mind, its own thoughts, which for the first time were not hers but its very own, rippling through him now and into her legs, which turned to jelly on his back.

"Turn him away from the ring," yelled Joe. "Take his eyes off it."

The stallion reared up as she tried to turn him, but she stayed with him. He pranced sideways, pulling hard and down on the bit.

Joe saw the panic in Elena's eyes as he rode toward her. She'd turned the stallion, but he still fought her, and Joe feared that if the horse turned back to the ring now, he would take off and the girl would never control him again. The horse could kill her in a second and he did not want to lose her for a dream.

When he got to her, the body of the mare seemed to quiet the stallion down. Elena got her horse to walk into the bit, then stand still.

"Tell me what to do," Elena said to her grandfather.

He heard the tremble in her voice. "You know what to do," Joe said.

"Yes, but I want you to tell me."

"Keep him quiet," Joe said. "Just make him stand."

Elena stared into the plains, the hills and sky, earth meeting heaven. She thought she would just ride out into it. She would take a mare, not this steaming, passionate animal filled with want, but a gentle, thoughtless horse, and just ride softly over the hills like a warm wind.

"You can't think it and do it," he said. "You just have to do it."

"I know," she said.

"You can't fall off," he said to her. "You can't fall off a horse."

"You can be bucked off," the girl said softly, "or thrown. But you can't fall off."

"Move in the saddle. Reins low. Indicate, don't steer. He'll take it from there. He knows what to do."

"Perch," said the girl, "don't ride."

"Kick outside, turn in, kick inside, turn out."

"Pull as you turn," she said, "in and down, all at once. Elbows in."

"Soft, smooth hands, don't jerk."

"Light on the reins, keep them low."

"You can't win if you knock down a barrel," Joe said.

"Ride with my body," she said.

"Fear him," he said.

The girl said, "No."

"Watch the barrels, not the horse," he said.

"Thank you, Grandpa. I'm ready." She turned the stallion and he crow-hopped twice, two short, quick bucks. She gathered him. She circled him to calm him.

"Ready?" said Joe.

"Yes," she said.

"All right," he said.

Then Elena sat back and, feeling the shift in her weight, the barrels coming into focus in front of him, the animal planted his strength into his hind legs. He shuddered. He exhaled. He stood as still as a rocket.

In that moment the world filled her. She became the wind on her cheek, she became the gentle creaking of leather as her weight rocked in the saddle. The world was silent and still. She was in ecstasy.

"Go!" her grandfather said.

Not stars, Joe thinks, but dreams. No, the darkness that erases daylight. No, a human heart for every star. He watches this girl breathing her thunder and thinks in that moment, No, it is death, not life, that is the dream. He watches time moving like a weightless pendulum, forward and back, back and forth. He is everywhere at once. He became aware, he was born, he became new at this moment and saw his grand-daughter riding. That was all. That was everything.

Elena was so much a part of the ride she could not experience it. She recalled herself both battering the earth and flying, she felt herself inside a roaring jet engine, in a tube of silence, she floated, she saw only the barrels, saw her grandmother riding beside her, riding inside her, she saw a plateau that became the sky. When she pulled up the stallion past the finish line, she could not separate his rumbling breath from her own, his strength from her own, his desire from her own. She watched her grandfather, who glanced at his watch and her miraculous speed.

"How fast?" she said.

"I forgot." He lied to her. "I lost track."

"Well, I'll do it again," she said.

"No," he said, "tomorrow. Enough for today. Go out and cool him off. I'm going to take care of the mares."

She let the animal out from underneath her and he stood calmly. He was hers again because he had done what he was born to do. Hers forever, she knew.

That night after she was asleep Joe went out to the corral to measure the distance between the barrels, the runway between the starting line and the corral, but he had not made a mistake. The distances were long enough, yet she had brought the horse in between fifteen and sixteen seconds. He told himself that of course barrel racing was 75 percent horse, maybe 80 percent. That the animal had been bred for it. That the girl was a good rider, a natural, light and lithe, and if anything she had been bred for it, too. Things happened. Unexplainable things occurred. Barrel racers came from somewhere, just like tennis players and gymnasts and ballet dancers. They were born. They occurred.

When he went back in, Elena was awake and waiting for him.

"I came in under sixteen," she said to him.

"Is that so?" he said. "How would you know that?"

"I saw the look on your face. And I can remember counting now, one thousand one, one thousand two. I counted pretty fast and I still came in under sixteen."

The old man nodded. He got the whiskey bottle and they shared a shot.

"I want you to come with me," she said to him. "I want you to come with me to the rodeos like you did with Grandma. And I need that horse. You know that, Grandpa. I need him."

"Finish your whiskey," he said to her, "and let's get some sleep."

"Grandpa," said Elena as she got into her sleeping bag on the floor. "Grandpa, what's your name?"

"Joe," he said.

"No, your last name. Mom's name before she was, you know, all her other names."

"Katsorus," he said. "Joseph Katsorus." He turned away from her. He poured himself a shot and drank it as he stared out the kitchen window toward the night sky.

"What is it?"

"What do you mean?" he said.

"What nationality? What country?"

"Greek," he said.

"Do Greeks like to ride horses?"

"Sure," he said. "Some of them. My father was a postman for a while. I remember the day he got fired, he was working a route that had our house on it. He delivered his own termination notice. The post office used horses back then. He didn't care for horses."

"Did your mother?"

"Yes. Before she married my dad. She was born in east Russia somewhere. Her family did a lot of riding."

"Why did she stop?"

"After my father lost his mail job he worked ore boats on the Great Lakes, later the docks. Horses take land, and money. Besides, they have a big national fair up in Toronto, the Canadian Exposition, and my father had to help unload some big horses. I don't quite know the story, but he ended up on the back of one and got thrown. Lost an eye. He was almost blind when he died."

"So you didn't have horses."

"No."

But Elena was thinking how it didn't matter. She felt as if she'd been alive forever, alive when the first human being crawled on the back of the first horse, alive when the first huge, hooved animal stretched itself across the plains, as if she had lived in the muscles of animals, of horses, of other beings. She felt the circle of life moving around the globe, westward from the plains of Asia in her great-grandmother's blood, eastward from China and down into the American plains through the Comanches, thousands and thousands of years distilling in her flesh. She had met the yellow stallion a thousand times, known him a thousand times, ridden him a thousand times.

The girl looked at her grandfather, still talking to her as he faced the window, a man who lived on the cusp of her lineage, a watcher and guide, not an avatar like her, but a soft reversal, a man in a garden, his wife dead, the snake in retreat, abandoned in paradise. His face reflected there in the dark pane, his eyes blank, his back silhouetted by stars, his shadow a penumbra of starlight. You could go back and back, she thought. You could go back forever.

He thought for the hundredth time what a silly man he was, of the foolishness of harnessing the will for anything but the moment. He thought, Embrace this gift.

He turned to her, reversing the play of light upon him, his face dark, his voice coming from the stars. "All right," he said.

A day could stretch forever. The sun sat still in the sky and lay down a yellow blanket of daylight on the plains. In the morning Elena rode the stallion around the barrels; in the afternoon she took him up into the hills, sometimes as far as the first stream. They cocked their heads in unison at the sounds of birds and the kiss of the wind. They listened for the herd, not knowing that her grandfather would not have let them up there alone if the horses were near.

She sat at the stream under a tree, the stallion feeding. She watched the clouds break above the tree branches, smelled the sweet air, felt the sun, put her feet in the cold stream. The horse came next to her to drink, mooching the water with his almost silent sucking, his warm, wet breath muttering at her neck.

Everything around her told her that all things lasted forever. She turned thirteen. On the way back, in the shadow-cast light, she took down a pheasant and brought it home.

For Joe, a day passed like a blink. In no time ten days had gone. Soon he would have to make his decision to confront the girl's mother, his daughter, to leave this place, at least for a time.

Of course, the girl could ride. She might be the best. He felt, himself, the thrill of her adrenaline. Watching her run the barrels almost brought him to tears. He knew it would convince the girl's mother, too. He'd seen her crying the night Elena first danced *The Nutcracker*, and the day she showed him the pictures of Elena prancing through her forms and receiving her red belt. She would not, in the end, argue with the quest for beauty and perfection. In the end, she, too, would give up all to give her daughter everything. Maybe she would sell the house in L.A. and get a ranch. She would encircle them with her love and make it so huge that Elena would find it wherever she ran.

He fell asleep that night in quiet expectation, bothered only by the strange, unnatural grinding of engines in the distance.

FIRE

In the morning, two boys on motorcycles came over the western slope. From the whine, Joe could tell the bikes had small two-stroke engines. They were customized for long, overland rides; he'd seen them before at some of the outfitters in Pinedale, oversize gas tanks and plastic reserve tanks straddled on back. With those engines and that much gas, if they wanted they could travel overland all the way to Kansas.

Elena came out and stood next to him, watching the boys come down over the hill, winding through the sage, the dirt flying from their wheels. Already the horses were edgy from the noise. The boys came up to the front of the cabin. They sat shirtless astride the bikes. They had short, moppy hair, shaved close to the head around the ears. The older, dark-haired boy's shoulders were covered with a baroque tattoo. The younger boy, a blond, wore a single small earring in his left ear. Their bodies were smooth and muscular, their skin tan beneath the layer of sweat and dirt. Elena caught the smell of gasoline as their eyes moved over her, and she fought the inclination to step behind her grandfather like a child.

"Turn them off!" Joe yelled, as the dogs ran at the boys, barking. "I can't hear you over the engines!"

The younger boy, the blond, flipped his key, but the older one grinned and revved his bike once, twice, before shutting it down.

"Where you from?" Joe said.

"Dogs," said the older boy. "What good?" He was a man, really, Joe could see that now. He must have been twenty-one or -two. But the younger one couldn't have been more than seventeen. "You own this land?"

"Some of it. Where you from?"

"This is way out here," said the older boy. "There's nobody out here."

"We're out here," said Elena, and the younger boy laughed. He had a nice laugh and a pretty smile. The older one frowned at him and the blond boy looked away, as if shy.

"I'm Wes," said the older boy finally, "and this is Dewey. Can we camp here?"

"Over the hill," said Joe, pointing toward the river. "Just don't run the machines by the horses. It spooks them."

"All right," said Wes. "If you're worried about it."

Dewey looked up as they started their bikes again. They were small bikes and they had to kick-start them. The boys straddled the machines, leaning them on their left legs, then lunging down with their right, the bikes bouncing under their weight and the engines whining to life as they flicked their wrists into the throttles.

The power of the gestures thrilled Elena.

Dewey grinned at her again, just a small half-grin, innocent, his face turned slightly away. She could not help but smile back.

Later, in the barn, as she readied the stallion, she read the worry on Joe's face. He surveyed the paddocks like a man preparing for an assault.

"You weren't friendly," she said to him.

"They aren't our friends," said Joe.

"They're boys," she said. "That's all."

"That's right," he said. He did not know how, or even if, he should tell her that Wes's tattoo was a prison tattoo. He'd seen them a hundred times on ex-cons. He did not know what to do with his fear, un-justified, because he felt that if a man served his time in jail, then he's spent his time; he did not have to live forever in jail. Men raped and murdered and never went to jail. Boys went in for puffing a marijuana cigarette.

They were young bucks, these two. And if they were not out here for trouble, he knew, too, that nei-ther did they care if they found it. A young girl, like Elena, was trouble. And how much trouble was an old man? He couldn't just box their ears.

And Elena, when she placed the bit in her stal-lion's mouth, felt for the first time something besides the exhilaration of the coming ride. The grinning boy. When she brushed down her horse's flanks she saw the boy's brown muscles. When she led the animal to the ring and he bowed to her, she backed away and saw the blond boy and his animal shyness.

For the first time, she rode poorly.

The boy walked over the hill. He came to the corral and watched.

Joe let the boy watch. He said nothing as Elena struggled with the stallion, turning in slow times and knocking over the barrels on her turns. Frustrated, Elena felt as if she would cry but for the boy watching. Joe told her to bring the animal in; then he closed the end gates and walked around to the girl and the horse.

"I was slow," Elena said.

"You were fighting each other," said her grandfather. "You can't fight about how you're going to go around those barrels." It was then he noticed that as she stroked the stallion's neck her eyes shifted to the fence and the boy. "Progress isn't linear," he said. "And you're going to have to learn to ride with an audience. Better take him out and cool him down now."

She took the stallion out the barn gate and Dewey walked toward them. The stallion stiffened and backed away when Dewey put out his hand.

"You ride pretty good," he said, not knowing what a good ride would be, but amazed, attracted, not even knowing why, by this girl who made the huge animal dance beneath her.

"I didn't today," she said.

"Do you think I could ride him?"

"No," she said. "I don't think he likes boys."

"You don't?" he said. He put his hand out to the stallion again and the animal backed away, snorting.

Elena turned her horse to circle him and he raised his hooves into a prance, dancing sideways, as Dewey backed into the fence, surrounded by the horse and young girl.

Elena laughed. "No, I don't think he does. Maybe Grandpa would let you ride a mare."

"Do you think?" he said.

"Maybe."

"He's your grandfather?"

"Yes. Have you ridden much?"

"No," he said.

"Then he won't let you," Elena said. She found her words coming easy. She thought the boy was funny, backed against the fence, afraid of her horse and wanting to ride. The stallion pranced away and she took him into a quick canter, stopped him, turned him. She felt powerful now, and she could not see that the boy felt that she needed him.

"Come tonight when I feed him. Maybe if you give him a carrot he'll let you touch him," she said. She turned the animal again and headed out, fast, though she knew she'd already worked him hard and should cool him down. She wanted to run. Needed to run. She would walk him back. She would let him walk and graze and they would soothe each other under the warm sun and mingling leather and sweat. She did not understand as she rode away from the boy the unnameable temptation in her power and speed.

Dewey came to the barn at dusk when she fed the stallion. He walked over the hill from his camp. Wes knew what he was about and had called him a fool.

"If you want that," he said to Dewey, "you just take it and we'll get the hell out of here."

"Fuck," said Dewey.

"What, you like her, Dewey? Want to marry her?"

"I'm going up to see the horse," said Dewey.

"Fuckin' idiot," said Wes.

Dewey sat on the hill in the fading light, positioning himself behind the sage so he couldn't be seen from the cabin, and waited for the girl to go to the barn. Then he went down.

When he came in the door the horse stirred and Elena turned.

"There's some old carrots in that barrel," she said. She pointed away from the paddock with her flashlight, to the back wall. "Over there."

Dewey went to the barrel and she walked over to him. She lifted the barrel lid for him and shined the light in at the carrots, but he stood there, dumbly. It made her think that maybe he was stupid, that there was something simple and brutish about him, even more simple than her horse. She reached in and got three carrots and held them out to him.

"Take them over to him," she said.

Dewey took the carrots from her hand. Now that she was down from the horse he saw that he was much bigger than she, and she felt it now, too, in the thickness of his rough-skinned fingers, in the same way that the delicacy of her bones made him feel, for the first time in his life, that his feelings for other girls had been mere abstractions of desire. At that moment Elena was thrilled with him. Thrilled with his attention. That he had come, without Wes, that he had watched and waited, as she knew he had to, to be here with her.

"Come on," she said.

But when he offered the horse the carrots, the stallion snorted and pranced away. She took the boy's hand and together they pushed the carrots into the paddock. She couldn't know the jealousies she stood between, the boy and the stallion.

"Maybe if I touch them, too," she said.

Her horse came forward and took the carrots then, quickly, like a dog, backing away immediately and letting them fall to the ground before eating them.

She went to the hay bales and got him some green hay.

"Is he yours?" asked Dewey.

"Maybe," she said. "I don't think he likes boys

so much." She walked away from the horse to the barn doors, and Dewey followed. She felt as powerful then as she did on the back of her horse, seeing the boy come toward her.

"What's your name?" he said.

"Elena."

"Can I kiss you?" he asked. He wanted everything from her, a kiss, a life. He wanted to crush her beneath him. He wanted to give up everything, get rid of her grandfather, and Wes, too, and stay here with her. He had lived on the streets in Denver. Been in reform school. Too much time in reform school; he barely knew girls, did not know what to do with a girl, but felt if she would give it, if she would let him have her, he would not have to take it. That would be better.

She watched this boy. She felt his hand tremble. She read it as weakness and felt sorry for him. She loved her stallion because he was not weak, because even at her command he held a deep part of himself away from her; he held his strength in check. This boy held something back, too, but she could not fathom it.

"Maybe," she whispered.

"Yes?" he said. "Maybe yes."

He lowered his face to hers and kissed her.

"Do you want to ride on my motorcycle?" he said.

"Not on the back. I want to drive it," said Elena.

"All right," he said. "Come in the morning. It likes girls."

She laughed. She did not expect him to be funny or quick.

He touched her chin and kissed her again. He

opened his mouth and she felt the soft inside of his lips. On the silk of his mouth the horse in the sky became a square of stars with sprawling arms, empty and figureless. Who could find a horse there now? In the vast, blank ether between those faceless suns?

When Elena went back to the cabin she told her grand-father that she did not want to ride in the morning. He realized it was not a bad day on the horse but something else.

"I can smell him on you," he said to her. "I can smell that boy."

She turned from him. She'd expected him to be like her parents, to know and not want to be told what they already knew.

"We only have two days left," he said. "What are you telling me?"

"Maybe the horse isn't everything after all," she said.

"No one ever said he was," said Joe, "except maybe you."

"Well, maybe I was wrong."

It didn't mean that she had to give it all up, that she'd wasted her time, but the last hour made her feel as if something had been lifted from her eyes and awakened inside her, that till now she'd been living in fairy dreams; even this horse, her dreams of the rodeo and barrel racing, seemed like the distractions of a child.

But he knew what she could not know. That she was a child. That she would have to make a big break for a little freedom. She would have to deny, to rupture, everything she had gained in a month for a few minutes with this stupid boy.

He'd seen it before. He'd watched his own daughter, the girl's mother, when her physical maturity turned to rage. This boy let Elena turn her back on her mother, her father, and now him, too.

He could allow that. He could take this month of his life that he'd filled with the rebirth of ghosts and hope, a month when he had turned around and redirected five years of solitariness. He could take it and put it away, turn around again to face his loneliness. Life and death had taught him enough to do that. But he could not let the girl risk her life.

The one thing he did not want was the return of jealousy and violence. And it had returned. It had come to his sanctuary. She brought it. He let it come.

That night he drank heavily for the first time in years. Life had made him a thoughtful man and a coward, but a million excuses weighed nothing against simple, necessary action. If he must, he would take on her hate. He would lose her forever. Give up everything. If there were one chance in a hundred, if there were any risk at all that she could be hurt, he would sacrifice his own life. In the morning he would make the boys go.

"Did you poke her?" said Wes.

"Kissed her," said Dewey.

"Kissed her."

"That's right," Dewey said.

"It doesn't matter, you know," said Wes. "It doesn't matter. Either way we're going to have to kill the old man or leave, so you may as well have poked her."

Dewey didn't say anything. It was always this way with Wes, some kind of ultimatum, some kind of choice that had to do with hurting somebody before they hurt you. He knew Wes was right, Wes just sometimes jumped the gun and started hurting before he had to.

Wes unrolled his blanket where he kept his rifle wrapped up. He ran the blanket up and down the dark gray barrel of the gun.

"You never killed anybody," Dewey said.

"You never poked anybody," said Wes.

"I did."

"Right," said Wes. "Somebody's butt in re-form school. You got that forty-four?"

"Yes," said Dewey.

"I never shot anybody in the face, you're right," Wes said. "But I shot them in the back from a car. It kills them all the same, you know."

"Gang-bangers use automatic weapons," said Dewey.

Wes raised the rifle and pointed it at Dewey's forehead. In the cramped little tent, that put it about an inch away. "You don't have to look them in the eye, Dewey," Wes said.

Dewey didn't want to talk about it anymore. He didn't believe Wes anyway. Anyway, he didn't want to believe him. He didn't want to shoot the old man. He didn't even want to take the girl. He wanted the girl to love him. That would make it easier and right.

"Jailbait, Dewey," said Wes. "Even for you." He brought the rifle back down. "Don't bring her down here, Dewey," he said. "You bring her down here and I'm going to poke her and let you watch and see how. Then we'll have to get out."

"You won't," said Dewey.

"Right," said Wes.

She awoke at the first light and dressed quietly as her grandfather slept. She'd thought it would be harder, and that failing to elude him she'd have to face him to go her own way. Adults took stands on the smallest things. They fell in love, had their hearts broken, had sex before marriage. She'd heard the stories. But when her time came Joe would stand between her and an innocent morning, learning to ride a motorcycle with a boy.

She would not have children, she thought, as she carried her boots outside the cabin door so as not to awaken him with her footsteps. She would not be like her mother.

Her grandfather slept so soundly. She had never seen him sleep like this, under the fist of liquor, his painful dreams wrestling with the harsh morning. She felt the cold wind sweeping in from the northwest. Winter clouds walked on the mountaintops, hung their purple veils on the dark cliffs ringing the valley. The slanting sunlight, barely gray, lay like gauze over their bleeding darkness.

Over the next ridge she saw the small tent inside a circle of gouged sage, the black fire pit smoldering. The tracks from the motorcycles cut swaths through the brush in jagged circles around the camp, unsymmetrical, patternless like the web of a black widow. She caught the smell of smoke and gasoline.

Dewey emerged from the tent in a patch of sunlight that moved swiftly and swirled beneath the waddling clouds. It was as if shadow and light danced down there in the ravine around the boy. She waved to him and he waved back. She descended.

He met her at the bikes, blowing on his hands, speaking in a whisper. "It's cold," he said. "Aren't you cold?"

She giggled. "No," she said. Standing next to the machines, she could almost feel their power running through her. "Do we each ride one?"

"No!" he said. He frightened her with his vehemence and she backed away. Seeing that, he glanced at the silent tent and then looked at her more softly. "No," he said again. "Nobody else rides Wes's bike."

He had no idea what he wanted to do, what he should do, but he thought maybe if he could get over the next ridge with her—he'd seen an abandoned shack not too far away—then they would be alone, far enough from her grandfather and from Wes.

"This one's yours," she said. She remembered from when they came in. Dewey had the blue bike, cleaner and newer. Wes's had a red gas tank, banged up from several falls and covered with silly decals of heavy metal rock bands.

Dewey put up the kickstand and grabbed the handlebars of his motorcycle. "Come on," he said, "let's walk it over here. I don't want to wake up Wes."

She followed him over to the other side of the fire.

"Okay," he said. "Get on."

"It'll fall over."

"You just stand over it," he said, "that's all."

He held the handlebars as she straddled the machine. It felt heavy and unyielding. The chill wind that swept over them seemed to ignite the machine with a bitter cold that crept into her hands and wrists.

Dewey had never taught anyone to ride, and all he could do was try to remember what he did when he got on and started the bike. "Sit down," he said.

"How do I start it?" said Elena.

"Sit down first. Keep your feet on the ground. I have to show you what everything is."

It was luck he had not anticipated. He got on the bike behind the girl and placed his arms along hers, his legs along her thighs. It felt warm and secure to her. His body guarded her from the wind and his hands seemed to take the chill off the handlebars.

"You brake with your right foot and right hand." He pressed the foot pedal and squeezed the hand brake and then she followed.

"This is the gas," he said, twisting the throttle at the right-hand grip. "That makes it go."

"That's easy enough," she said.

He leaned to the other side, moving his lips over her other ear. She felt him tighten and his breath quicken.

"Don't worry," she said, thinking to soothe his nervousness. She was capable. She wouldn't hurt his bike.

He grabbed the clutch on the left side. "You pull this handle in to shift. You got to have it in to start."

"All right."

"And you shift with your left foot. Down for first gear, one up for every one after. You start in first. You got that?"

She did not get it. She did not quite understand gears, but now they were too far along and she was afraid to tell him. He seemed too close to her, too big, too warm. His lips brushed against her hair and she felt him hardening against the seat of her pants.

"Let's start it," she said.

"Well, maybe I should get it going and ride us around a bit to get you used to it."

"No," she said, "I want to go."

He was afraid that he would lose her, that she would leave, and he did not want that.

"Okay," he said. "Hold the clutch in. Kick the kick-start and rev and gas at the same time. Then just let the clutch out."

For the first time she was afraid. She did not know how to drive the machine, which she suddenly found complicated and uncompliant. She was afraid of the boy, who had become hot and insistent, his voice intolerant, his hardness pressing against her. She did not know if it was his heartbeat she felt in his stiffened penis or if he was pushing his hips rhythmically into her. In her panic she wanted to get away, but she felt trapped on all sides, as much by the admonishment of her grandfather as the overtures of the boy.

She pulled in the clutch and slammed down on the kick-start, kicking Dewey in the shin. He yelled as the machine miraculously leaped to life, filling the valley with a shrill cry that seemed to silence everything, even the wind.

Shocked, she yanked at the throttle and opened the clutch in one fast jerk, which sent the bike forward, the front wheel jumping into the air, the back pushing under it, the bike flying up, throwing both riders to the ground. It landed harshly near them, as if dead, and in her daze she could not tell if it had hit her or if she had escaped.

"Idiot!" he yelled, and she rolled from him, hurt in a hundred ways.

She felt a bolt of pain in her right ankle and shin as she tried to stand up and the leg collapsed underneath her. She lay there, watching the seething boy crying over his machine, unconcerned about her leg. Then Wes emerged from the tent.

He surveyed the scene quickly and moved toward Elena. He was so fast she found his movement incomprehensible as he pounced at her, grabbing her by the armpits and dragging her toward the tent.

"Dewey!" she yelled. "Dewey!" She knew instinctively now what her grandfather had warned. She felt it in the hard digging of Wes's fingers into her armpits. She yelled again, "Dewey!" but Dewey stood dumb-faced. She tried to struggle. If she could get to her feet she could fight him, but Wes put her in a headlock as he dragged her, his arm under her throat.

"Little bitch," said Wes. "I told you, Dewey."

And Dewey watched. He looked on, accepting, as he often did with Wes, now that his moment had passed and things would go on, inevitably, as they always did, however cruelly. He wondered if he could face the girl when Wes was done with her. Maybe she would be out cold, or he could soothe her and befriend her again.

Elena knew now that Dewey would not help her. If she could get to her feet, if her leg would hold her, she could pull Wes by the hair or elbow him in the gut, she could get free to kick him and run, but he forced her down as he dragged her. She twisted, grabbing his leg, and bit him above the knee, but he yanked her down by the hair. He put his hand on her throat. "All right now," he said. He ripped her T-shirt away with his free hand, then went to her pants. She screamed, "Dewey!" knowing he would do nothing, screaming in rage for her knowledge of it.

Wes came down on her, his knee between her legs. She remembered then that her hands were free. If she could get a finger into his eye—he hit her across the face. She began to cry as he rose up again, his hand over her. And then a shot broke the air. A second one sent a metal pot on the fire circle dancing.

Wes stopped.

"If you don't think I can hit you from here, you're wrong," Joe said. He began to walk down the hill, slowly, the scoped rifle cocked near his shoulder. He'd awakened after dawn, and, finding Elena's bed empty, went to the barn. When he did not find her with the horses, he got the rifle and he headed for the camp, but was only halfway there when he heard the girl screaming.

Elena scrambled up, the pain in her shin disappearing as she ran up the hill to her grandfather. He lowered the gun. Wes stood. Joe raised the gun again.

"To the side!" Joe yelled to her, waving her away.

She wanted to run up to him, to hide behind him. He kept the rifle on his shoulder and put his hand out to her. He squeezed her hand gently. "Walk behind me," he said.

They came down and Joe stopped within ten yards of the boys.

"Get out now," he said.

"It looks like rain," said Dewey. He did not look at Elena, who kept her own head high, looking for Dewey's eyes. She wanted to find sympathy, sorrow, in them. She knew he'd been a coward, but she could forgive his cowardice. She wished, even in her fright, to see something in him that understood her pain.

"It'll take us a while," Wes said. Nothing had changed for him but the fact that the old man held a gun. Everything depended on that.

"Now," Joe said. He shifted the rifle at the bikes. "You'll ride out now or you'll walk out a little later."

The boys broke camp. They took down the tent and hid their guns in their bedrolls. They packed the bikes. They did not look at Joe or Elena. They mounted the machines, started them, and rode out as the clouds merged over the sun and the first of the blue rain dripped from the sky.

Joe put his arm around the girl as he watched the boys drive through the sage to the east.

Elena hugged him. Now that the bikes were gone she felt the cold rain and heard the droplets puttering onto the dust.

"Grandpa," she said, crying. "Grandpa."

"It's all right," he said softly, telling her the greatest of all the lies he knew. "It's all right."

WATER

It rained and rained. He could not remember it raining so hard, but Joe told Elena there was nothing to fear, not in the torrential rain, not in the lightning, not in what the girl called "the wicked thunder."

"The prairie has been here a long time," he said.

"But people have come and gone," said the girl.

"We have the boat, the truck, the horses if we need them," he told her.

"We don't even have a radio," she said.

There was no reason to have a radio. There was nothing to get on the radio.

"We have a phone," he said.

He dressed Elena's wound, a bloody scrape down the length of her shin. He wrapped her sprained knee in an elastic bandage. It began to hurt again, now that the danger had passed, but he told her she would have to get up and around; he needed her to help stabilize the outdoor shed for the mares and bring in the stallion.

They were soaked the moment they emerged from the cabin. The mares seemed to sway between lethargy and panic, standing quietly in the rain. Then, cautiously approaching the shed, they burst into furious, short gallops when it teetered and creaked in the wind. She helped her grandfather carry boards from the barn that he nailed at angles from the shed's roof beams to the frame. The water battered at the aluminum roof like bombs as she helped him lay down a flooring of straw under the structure. If the animals came under, they would not have to stand with their ankles deep in mud.

She wondered at the mistrust of these animals who had known Joe for most their lives. Even in the hellish downfall of water she stopped to marvel at their deep simplicity, the self they kept hidden, that part of them, their souls, that kept them flying across the plains as they quietly stood.

"Come on, dream girl," Joe said. "Let's get that stallion in."

And the mares, once she and her grandfather left the corral, slowly moved to the shed.

Outside his paddock her stallion raged at the rim of his corral, as if to create a storm within that would match the fury of the one without.

"I don't know how to get him in," said Joe. "But if we don't we could lose him."

Elena said nothing. She went to the stall and climbed onto the bottom rung, extending her hands to the seething horse, who stood still when he saw her, immense, the lightning ripping the mountaintops behind him. He walked to her and put his nose in her hands.

"I guess he's mine," Elena said.

"More like you're his," said Joe.

He circled them and closed the doors to the stall. The girl fed her stallion carrots, wiped the water from his back, and brushed him down. She fed him dried alfalfa. Then she and her grandfather went back through the rain, beneath the black sky, to the cabin, where they dried off. He lit a fire on the woodstove and boiled water for tea.

"I need whiskey," the girl said.

"No," he said, "we don't need whiskey. The last thing you need, when you need whiskey, is whiskey."

"For the pain," she said.

"What pain?" he said. "I'll get you some aspirin."

"Because everything has changed. I did the wrong thing and changed everything," said Elena. She began to cry a little now. She began to feel like the sky, full of fullness, full of pain, full of the fullness of pain.

"Nothing has changed but you," said Joe. He went to the stove and pulled the teapot, lifted the lid and added two tea bags, then closed the lid again. He lit a lantern as the wind pounded the cabin in gusts of rain that spattered through the western cabin wall. "If I hadn't of got drunk last night, I would have been awake this morning and stopped you. I would have made them leave anyways. You would have been safe and hated me for it."

She did not know what to do with that truth. All this time she had begged for simple truth and now, after a day of it, she was exhausted by it.

"I'm sorry, Grandpa," she said.

He put a blanket on her shoulders and poured them tea.

She began to cry now. Till then it had been too

133

much, but now, feeling the cruel weather, she realized she would not get to ride again. The rain would let up and her parents would come. She would have to leave. More than anything that happened with the boys, it was the loss of this life and its freedom, the loss of the stallion, that tore at her. "I don't want to leave," she said.

"You'll ride him," he said to her. "I'll bring him to you." Because he felt then as he had not felt since he'd seen his own daughter crying, since his wife lay her head on his shoulder and whispered, "Remember me." In the end, he thought, it came down to unkept promises and regret, to death and memory, and this clinging to the moments in between. He would do anything for this child. Anything.

They sat quietly in the hard-falling night, under the blistering storm, the thunder pounding, the rain covering everything.

She thought of the river below them, swelling with rain, the swollen earth, her horse of stars running free above the clouds, above the deluged world.

He thought, as he prepared for bed, that we are battered by what we cannot accept until we accept it all.

She thought of her yellow horse, his black mane, his dark eyes turning back the lightning, facing with calm the rage of the storm.

Joe did not expect them to return. Not in this rain. But they did. Hidden by the thunder and cloudburst, their engines inaudible until the gunshots whacked the night and splintered the cabin walls. He was wounded, his right leg burst open at the thigh before he was even awake.

What luck, he thought, what bare luck to hit him through the cabin wall.

Elena leaped up as if she had been dreaming of their return, though she had been dreaming of her stallion. She yelled, "The horses!" Throwing on her pants and boots and running to the door.

He did not want to tell her he was hurt, to frighten her, but as his head cleared and more shots rang out, the buzz of the motorcycle engines sifting through the maelstrom of noise and his pain, the blood on his hands, he yelled to her, "No!" but too late.

Out the door the rain blasted at her, she could

see nothing, and ran from memory to the corral and barn. She fell in the mud. She knew her grandfather could hold them off with his gun, but she also knew the minds of these boys who, riding their fear and vengeance, would shoot at the animals to kill them. If she released the mares now, they would return at the end of the storm.

She heard the whine of the engines in the dark, but she could not see the motorcycles as she got up and ran to the corral and pulled out the back fence that opened to the plains. She ran in, shooing the mares, who thundered around her reluctantly, then advanced in a single, quick swerve to the opening and headed back into the black prairie.

Joe fell from his bedroll. He crawled first to the phone, which he found dead. It did not matter now whether it was the boys or the storm who cut it off. He tried to stand, but fell, as his leg broke under him, the blood gushing out with his heartbeat, the white, shattered bone opening through his skin in a flower of blood. He felt the cold white wave of unconsciousness sweep at him, which he fought with his nausea and dizziness. He tried to gather himself to crawl for his rifle.

If Elena could get back to the cabin safely and if he could get to the rifle, then she'd have done the right thing. The boys would shoot the horses if they could. If she set the animals free they would return to the ranch after the storm. The boys probably did not know about the boat or the truck. Whether bullies or cowards or even murderers, they probably would prefer to avoid a face-off with guns.

As he lay there, putting it together, fighting his dizziness, he heard the engines disappear behind the beating rain. He waited as the ceiling beams swirled in a whirlpool above him. He should stop the bleeding. He should get his rifle. He should check on the girl. But he felt too weak to move. He listened to the storm.

It seemed the boys had come and gone. Reckless vandals, they'd done their thoughtless damage, made their devilish run. He worried about Elena, how she would deal with his wound. He breathed deeply and gathered himself, thinking of how to wrap the leg, but thought it better to get the rifle first just in case. He pushed forward again toward the rack near the kitchen, but did not get far before Wes and Dewey came through the door.

He wondered how visible was his despair. Dewey stood stupidly with his six-gun, but Wes surveyed the cabin like a predator, his head, shoulders, rifle poring quickly over the room. He went to the gun rack and grabbed the rifles, made sure they had no clips in them, and then threw them out the door into the mud. Now Wes held the gun. It changed everything for Wes now that he held the gun, and he stared down upon Joe with the despicable arrogance of this reversal.

"Watch him," Wes said to Dewey. "I'll get the girl."

Though the rain still smashed through the sky as the mares fled, beating upon her and the earth, the quieting of the machines felt like silence. She wondered if she should have let the animals go at all. They'll come back, she thought. They'll return. She listened to the pattering rain, felt positive, powerful, capable, taking care of the horses, wet in the storm.

Soaked, she decided to check on the stallion before going back to the cabin. She walked through the mud of the corral and through the rain. It was then she saw the dogs lying dead. She could not think of them now. She could not even think of the boys. They were gone again. There was work to do. She would think about things later. Talk with Joe about it next to the fire.

Near the barn now she could hear her animal, his screaming and the thud of his hooves against the dirt. She entered the building puzzled, worried, as she saw the stallion's feet flung into the air, his head twisting vehemently at the haystack next to the door. Then she felt the arm around her throat.

She knew from the morning, from the acidity of his sweat and the bulk of his muscles, that it was Wes, but since then she had remembered his attack already a hundred times. She quickly lowered her elbow into his ribs, which caused him to loosen his grip. Before he could tighten again she had his wrist, twisting it down and away, then up again, against the natural motion of his shoulder. She broke his grip, turned him, and spun from him, but she was too close to snap-kick him in the groin, so she rolled into him with a roundhouse to his ribs. It was not her best but it was enough to get away. He backed up, startled. But he was too strong to be much hurt.

He was huge. She saw that now. And there was no place to run. She had her back to her muttering stallion as Wes cut off the only open door. She thought to run through the stallion's paddock and try to escape through his corral, but seeing Wes's rifle leaning against the far wall, she feared putting the stallion between herself and her attacker.

Wes breathed heavily, his exhalations like train whistles. She heard the rain. And a shot from the direction of the cabin. She knew the sound of the Rugers and it was not that sound.

Wes heard it, too, and broke into a small grin. "All right now," he said as he came toward her again. "All right."

Joe preferred to die stoically if he must die. He would not beg for his life, but he would beg for his granddaughter's. He tried to breathe deeply enough to stay the pain in his thigh, to fight the waves of shock and nausea, to stay conscious. Unconscious, he was worth nothing. And everywhere the horrid drumbeating wind and rain and here, in front of him, this silent boy with a gun.

"This ends nowhere, Dewey," said Joe. "You've done your damage."

"I'm waiting for Wes," said Dewey.

"More could be too much trouble," Joe said. "Just get out now. Go."

"I'm waiting for Wes," said Dewey.

Joe began to crawl toward him and Dewey backed up. If his crawling toward him made Dewey back away, it said something about his unwillingness. Slowly, Joe sat up.

"Just wait for Wes," Dewey said. "We'll see what Wes says." He edged backward again slightly, and Joe pulled himself up on his left knee.

"Wait for Wes!" said Dewey.

But now Joe stood. "Dewey," he said. He limped forward one step and Dewey lowered the muzzle and fired the gun.

Wes came at her slowly, confidently. He did not seem worried.

"Learned a few tricks back home after grade school, I guess," he said. "I hope all your homework was done." He stepped toward her. "I know those tricks," he said. He whispered, "I was in prison a long time learning tricks."

As she backed toward the corral everything seemed so quiet. She had a thousand thoughts and a thousand years to think them. She worried about her parents and if they would be able to get up to the Winds through the heavy rain. She wondered about Joe and how lonely he would be when she left. She thought about Dewey and the softness of his lips and how he had made her forget everything. Poor Dewey, she thought, stuck out here with Wes. She saw Wes stepping toward her in infinitely long moments, each divided, each slow. She felt as if it were impossible for him to reach her.

"Why?" she said to him.

"Being dead," he said. "I've been dead; it's not so bad." He put out his hand. "Come here," he said. "You can do it and get beat up, or you can just do it."

She lived in L.A. Her mother had said, "If you're cornered they will beat you anyways; you'll get killed anyways, so be quick and do what you can." Wasn't that silly? What would anyone want from her?

"Don't hurt my grandpa," she said.

"No," said Wes. "I won't." He came forward and she put her hand out to him. She heard the rain again. "All right now," he said. "That's good. That's right." He took her hand.

She pulled his arm toward her and quickly twisted it, bringing his elbow down backward on her knee. She heard the crack of his bones snapping at the pressure point. He yowled horribly, but he was too strong and quickly spun away, crying and screaming, "You bitch, you fucking bitch!" He backed to the doorway, where his rifle was propped against the wall of the barn. He picked it up and cradled it in his left arm, pulling it up to his shoulder. Tears poured from his eyes in anger and humiliation.

"First the horse," he said. "You little bitch. First your horse."

But she ran at him, reaching his chest and pushing him back. His shot blasted into the air. He spun, hitting her shoulder with the rifle and knocking her to the ground where he had her now, at his feet. He kicked her away from him. He lowered the gun. And she imagined how she looked underneath him, at the end of the gun barrel. She saw her own innocent eyes, sincere and questioning, looking at death and infinity, as clueless and wide-eyed as a wounded bird.

But the gunshot brought the pacing stallion to his crest. The boy did not even see the animal raise his hooves and bring down the fence, but turned only when he heard the horse come crashing through. The stallion was upon him before he could spin and fire.

The animal knocked Wes to the ground and brought its powerful feet down on Wes's chest. He did not even have time to scream. Elena heard only the deadly thud of the stallion's hooves upon muscle and flesh. Wes turned his shoulder up and tucked his knees, but the horse rose again and came down furiously on the boy's head, crushing his skull. Wes writhed, his arms and legs flailing out madly, but he was beyond pain when the horse continued to rain his hooves upon him, stomping his limbs into quiet. Then Elena's stallion turned and backed away from the boy's body. He did not even look at the girl, but broke out into the storm, through the open doors of the barn and into the night.

*　*　*

Dewey did not know how to handle a gun well, and the kick from the pistol, aimed at Joe's head, made the shot go wide and high. But it stopped Joe.

"I told you!" said Dewey. "I told you!"

Joe backed away. "I'm going to sit, all right?" he said.

Dewey watched him closely, as if, Joe thought, he were something dangerous and not a wounded old man. If not for Elena, he would not have prolonged this absurd death, but made the boy kill him. That's what he told himself until he heard Wes's rifle from the barn. He did not know whether to hope the boy had shot the horse. He did not know, at this point, in what way the girl could be worse off.

"Why don't you do it, Dewey?" he said. "Why wait for Wes?"

"What!" said Dewey.

"Does Wes have to do everything? Can't you just kill me?"

"Don't make me mad," said Dewey.

Joe collapsed. He thought he would cry, but would not do it in front of this idiot boy. "Dewey," he said, convinced now that he would die anyway from the wound, wondering if he had taught Elena enough, if by chance she survived this, if she knew enough to survive more. "Dewey, I'm trying to make you mad."

It was then that he saw the girl in the doorway, standing with Wes's gun. She'd looked inside and backed away. Dewey, seeing Joe focus on the doorway, turned, but finding nothing, turned back quickly again.

Joe did not know what Elena could do. But she held the rifle now. She held her universe in her own hands.

Joe looked at the floor, averting his eyes from

the doorway as he slid sideways to get out of the line of fire.

"What are you doing?" said Dewey.

"Just getting out of the wind," Joe said.

Dewey watched him. Joe met the boy's eyes. There was nothing now but the rain and wind, a flash of lightning, and seconds later its thunder.

"It should be on top of us in a while," said Joe.

Dewey watched him.

Joe shifted. He wanted the boy to watch him. "Storm should be right on top of us in a little while."

"Shut up," said Dewey, almost pleading. "Please shut up."

Elena had expected to find Dewey, and that's why she took Wes's lever-action Marlin. The magazine still had two bullets in it. She hadn't thought what she might do. She thought she could protect herself, and if she had to, protect her grandfather, if he were still alive. Now she saw him, his right leg stretched out stiffly, the huge gash, a hole of blood and sinew in his thigh.

The boy who'd kissed her only the night before stood over him. She did not feel anything like vengeance or hate. If Dewey were not holding a gun she'd take him captive. Then she would use the phone and call for help. But as her grandfather had taught her, there were a million things to think and only one or two that she could do. She put the rifle on her shoulder and stepped into the doorway.

Whether it was a look from Joe, or whether he heard her shuffle, Dewey again felt the presence at the door. But, embarrassed by his last skittish twisting, he glanced over his shoulder only furtively, seeing the figure, thinking at first it was Wes, then realizing that it was not, turning slowly, infinitely slowly, toward the girl, his gun now raised again to fire.

She'd wished deep in her heart that she could have taken him blindly. Shot him in the back of the head. But he turned toward her and she saw Dewey's eyes, the eyes of a boy, as stupid and as gentle as a doe. It was with this gentleness that she squeezed the trigger, shot him in the forehead, took him down.

"Help me to the bed," her grandfather said. There were things to be done and much, he thought, that Elena did not need to contemplate.

She pulled him under his armpits as he pushed himself backward across the floor with his good leg. She noticed the splattering of bone and blood from the back of Dewey's head on her grandfather's chest. In any other circumstance the bloody explosion of her grandfather's wound alone would have nauseated her, weakened her too severely, but everything seemed to swirl now, as if the dire nature of the events made death unthinkable and the necessities of survival as ordinary as the ticking of a clock. She got him to his bed.

"Pack the wound with mud," he said. That was all. Then, finally, he let himself pass out.

She found a towel and the first-aid kit, which contained a bit, not nearly enough, of gauze and medical tape. She did not know anything about cleaning the wound, which still bled, but she followed her grandfather's advice. She stepped over Dewey and went outside, where she gathered mud in the cup of her hands and brought it in, in three trips covering the wound. She tried to smooth it flat, like a plaster, to cover it, to end it. She put the towel over her work and tried to wrap it with the tape. Then she propped up the leg. She found the whiskey and the aspirin and put them next to him as the center of the storm broke over the ridge in a simultaneous blast of lightning and thunder and a horrible downpour, which roared against the cabin walls and roof.

She turned to the dead boy and grabbed his feet. Struggling with his weight, she dragged him to the door. She'd thought to drag him to the barn with Wes, thinking that once she got him outside, the slipperiness of the mud would make pulling him easier, but he was too heavy, and she hadn't calculated that she, too, would slip in the mud. She fell, slipping under his legs, which were still loose and warm. "I'm sorry, Dewey," she said, and gave up the task as impossible, leaving him outside the door.

Her grandfather was burning up with fever now, so she fetched a washcloth, soaked it with cold water, and placed it on his head the way her mother did for her when she had the flu. She sat with him. She sat with him as the rain poured down on the prairie, relentless, and the thunder and wind swept over everything.

He awoke only once and she sat him up and gave him aspirin and whiskey. He sputtered, but finally took it down.

"How do you feel, Grandpa?" she said.

He tried to speak, but he was too weak. A world of things whirled inside his fever and he wanted

146

to say them all. They were all important things, but somehow he could not line them up. He felt as if the palm of death were closing around him and he wanted to scream, but the puffy fist of unconsciousness covered his mouth, suffocating him, and again he lost touch.

She laid him back down. She sat with him through the night, opening his bandage and daubing the wound with mud, brushing his head with the cold cloth, listening to his hot muttering, sounds without meaning or sense.

She tried the phone, but found it dead. She went outside with a flashlight and found that the phone wires had been cut. She had no idea how to fix them. Around the front of the cabin she retrieved her grandfather's rifles from the mud. There was one round left in Wes's Marlin, but she did not want to look for bullets on his body or use his gun. Under the storm, next to her grandfather's bed, she cleaned the mud from the guns, then took them apart, dried them, and oiled them and reassembled them as her grandfather had taught her.

The black rain came and came and did not let up. But she told herself that it could not rain forever, that the night would end, that light must come, that all things change, and there would be dawn, and morning, and that her grandfather would awaken and then they would get to work.

He did awaken with the gray light that crept into the valley and sat under the clouds and rain and never got lighter. He got up on his elbow, stiffly, and blinked.

"How do I look?" he said.

"Gray," she said.

"Gray. Gray is not a good color for a human being."

"You're fever's down," she said to him. "I was afraid you'd die."

"Me, too," he said. He did not mention that he still feared it. "Still raining."

"Yes."

He looked at the floor.

"I put him outside," Elena said. She told him about the stallion, and Wes, that the phone wires were cut and the horses gone.

"Did you look for the motorcycles?" he asked. "Can you ride one?"

"No," she said. "No. You couldn't ride one."

"You could," he said.

"No," she said.

"Well," he said, "we'll check them." He told her she'd have to go to the barn and get some wood and twine to make a splint for his leg. Could she go back in there?

"Yes," she said.

She'd have to fetch the rifles. They could take one and use the other as a crutch.

She showed him the cleaned guns.

"Well," he said, smiling for the first time.

She bent down and hugged him. "I love you, Grandpa," she said. "We're going to be okay."

"We'll hike down to the boat, take it across, and drive out of here," he said. "Now get the wood."

She helped him tighten the bandage and build the splint. He did not tell her that he felt so weak he did not think he could stand, let alone hike to the boat, but they would take it a step at a time. At some point, if needed, he would release her to go get help.

They packed some jerky and water, their knives, matches, took the scoped rifle, all of which she carried. Then she helped him up. The Ruger was short and he had to hold the stock in his hand to get even leverage, but he stood. He felt the blood rush out of his head and into the wound, and she saw him teeter and go white. But he held. He put his left arm over her shoulder and they staggered out into the rain.

The gun barrel sank in the mud and twice they slipped and fell, once going up the hill and again coming down in the next ravine. They passed the motorcycles at the bottom of the next ridge, drowned now in mud, their twisted handlebars protruding cold and skeletal into the rain, and he marked their location. Halfway up the last ridge he had to stop, and his granddaughter held him up as the weakness ran through him. He held in his bowels, but felt the heat of urine in his pants and for the first time thanked God for the rain.

In all the misery, she felt pleasure in helping him, his arm around her, needing her. She felt a tremendous confidence sweeping through her now as the rain pelted them on the side of the hill. She fed him with her strength and heat.

"Okay, Grandpa," she said, "one last push."

He gripped her and the two of them climbed. They rose to the top of the hill to gaze down on the river. There, they found that the river had flooded its banks. The boat was swept away, the road gone, the truck underwater.

"We have to go back," said her grandfather.

"Can you make it?"

"I'll have to," he said.

After all she had been through, for the first time she was worried. She wasn't sure he could make it back to the cabin. His eyes were glassy and his voice a whisper. Despite his outlook, which often seemed joyless, his face, his voice, always emitted hard determination. Now, he seemed little and old; the croak in his voice sounded like something breaking.

"Your leg, Grandpa," she said to him. "Can you wait it out?"

"We can't wait it out," he said. If the river were this high, then the levee east of Pinedale would give out, if it had not already. These ravines, open to the full force of the storm, would pay the price in a flash flood. Everything would be swept away. He told her this. "We have to get to high ground," he said.

He regretted all the precautions he'd never taken, living alone, waiting for nothing but the next day. A raft. Who would need a raft in the mountains? A tent. He seldom camped and when he did he did not go far; he slept under the stars or rode back to the cabin when it rained. But it did not take much for everything to go wrong and leave him in this back-wash of guilt and regret. How would he protect this child?

"It's too wet and cold," the girl said. "What will we do?"

"I don't know," he said. "First things first. First the high ground, shelter later."

He turned and sat, starting down the hill by sliding on his butt. She took the Ruger from him and walked next to him helplessly. The sky came down upon them, brooding, swollen. It seemed impossible that it could rain harder, but it did. The air was a sheet of driving rain. At the bottom of the hill he looked wearily at the sodden motorcycles, but even if he had the strength to get to them, to help her start one, if that were even possible, he would still have to get to high ground and he could not do it without her. Nor would she leave him.

He stood up and put his arm over her. He felt heavier to her than before. Colder. They stopped a half dozen times, fell twice, before making the top of the ridge. The mud was thick and flowing and every-where. The thunder rolled over the eastern mountains and the echo came back upon them. The air was so filled with dark that the lightning barely penetrated. Most of all, there was the constant rain, drowning everything.

She followed him again as he slid down the hill toward the cabin. At the bottom, she helped him in-side. He lay on the floor, shivering, his lips blue.

"Grandpa," she said. "Grandpa." She began to cry.

Her sobbing brought him to consciousness.

"Don't cry," he said. "Put as much food as you can in your pack." He gasped for breath. He could not tell if he were dying or just tired. He'd thought if he were dying he could tell, but he could not. "Make sure you have your knife, the gun, dry matches, water, and food."

"Yes," she said. She gathered what she could. "We should wait," she told him. "You need to rest."

"The flood will kill us," he whispered. "Go to the barn and get your horse's bridle."

"He's gone," she said. "Grandpa, all the horses are gone."

"Darlin'," he said to her. "I'm not delirious just yet. You might need it. Get the bridle."

She ran through the rain. The boys lay dead on the ground, Dewey outside the cabin door, Wes in the barn. In the barn, dry and warm and full of the smell of her horse, she felt as if nothing had changed. She went to the wall and took down her stallion's bridle. She smelled the mink oil she'd lathered into its leather only a day or so before, before the boys came, before the rain. It reminded her of then, before all this, and she thought, it could very well be like that, that really nothing had changed and nothing bad could happen. The world, with its impending danger and tragedy, fell away.

When she got back to the cabin her grandfather was sitting up. He had some strength back in his eyes. It struck her that the danger was possibly overblown. If they could get to high ground, they would be safe. If the ravine didn't flood, they could return to the cabin. If not, then they would be wet, that's all. Her grandfather would survive the wound. He was not dying, but in pain. The rain would stop. Her parents would be coming for them.

"All right," he said. "Maybe we can find a cave back up there."

She helped him up and he put his arm over her shoulder. He, too, had regrouped. It did not matter if he were dying or not, to act as if he were dying would accomplish nothing. He smiled at his granddaughter.

"Let's get out of here," he said.

The first hill was not so steep, but neither was it high enough to get them out of the ravine. They had to go down again and she followed him as he slid. More than half the day was gone now. It was already late afternoon. The longer they survived, the better the chance that someone would come.

Resting there at the bottom of the ridge, again he looked far too weak to move. His hands shook and he breathed unevenly. His right leg was stiff and useless. He himself could not tell the difference between his shivering and burning. At times the leg felt like a toothache, at times a fire, and other times as if it were not there at all, but already dead. Ten feet up the ravine he collapsed.

In the distance, to the west, she heard an unusual roar, and when she turned to him he came awake again. He made no sound, but she read his lips, which were dry and purple even under the deluge. "It's coming," he said.

Because he could no longer stand, she tried to drag him by his armpits up the ravine. He pushed with his good leg at first, but soon weakened and fainted and she collapsed underneath him. Now the ominous rush of the approaching flood filled her as she got down on her knees to lift him onto her back.

Her survival pack was in the way and she had to take it off. She abandoned his gun and the bridle.

She could not get the pack over his shoulders, so she left it, too, but she managed to slip the shoulder strap of the second Ruger over his arm. She buckled the canteen to his belt, pocketed the matches, checked for her own knife, and slid herself under him. In that way, she began to crawl with him up the hill.

It became a dreadful and eternal crawl. She dragged herself with him on her back, sometimes not even on hands and knees, but dragging them both along on her stomach, pulling herself forward by grabbing at the stalks of the chaparral. The top of the hill came no closer at all. The rain came down, relentless. She breathed water and mud, her grandfather's warm, dead weight pressing into her. Unconscious, he slid from her back and she adjusted, keeping her weight underneath his. She felt his trembling breath in her ear, his heartbeat on her back. She held to those things now, his breath, his heart, as if they were all the world. They meant everything. She crawled. She saw herself on the back of her horse, the yellow stallion, his black mane and tail flying, his green eyes eating up the ground. She felt his thunder coming through her. She rode him to the top of the ridge and into the starlit sky.

Then, in a moment, she is not upon him, but beneath him. Her foot is caught in the cinch and his hooves pound around her head, her chest and face drag across the ground. She is screaming for her father. She is screaming and screaming.

She crawled up the hillside in the mud and rain, carrying her grandfather. She heard him speak. He whispered, "Water," and she did not know if he spoke of the water in the air or the coming flood, if he needed a drink or a place to rest his soul. She slid him from her back and opened the canteen to his lips.

He gasped. "Not far now."

"No," she said, though it seemed infinitely far. She felt the demons of regret in the air around her and in the heavy rain, which could wash nothing away.

"Not far," he said. There were so many things he wanted to think. How did he get here? It was a sloppy path to heaven, even on the back of a child. He thought of his wife. If he missed one thing the most, it was her heat in the middle of a cold and rainy night. The paradise of her arms. How many times had she held him in that once endless past? He'd thought love could never end. Then it ended. He once thought everything ended and he now thought nothing had an end.

Elena lifted her grandfather and moved beneath him again. As she crawled on her stomach in the mud, she felt the explosion of urine and feces on her back. Not knowing what it meant, she was glad for the heat still inside him. Slowly, she moved up the ridge in the rain, and finally she reached the top of the hill.

It seemed lighter up there. The rain less heavy, the sky almost pale. She placed her grandfather next to her and sat in the rain. She heard the roar of water in the west and saw the giant wall of mud and debris sweep into the ravine, engulfing the ranch, the cabin, the barn and corrals, filling the valley, swallowing it whole. In a moment, everything was gone. A month. A life. She knew that farther down the tide would sweep away the abandoned shack of the Mormon boy, and the ghost ranch, and anything else beyond. Everything swept under the torrent. Everything gone.

"Grandpa," she said, shaking him. "Grandpa, look."

But the old man did not move. His lips had stopped trembling. He had no breath or heartbeat in his chest.

She knew that he was dead. She sat in the storm, alone in the mountains of Wyoming. Nothing around but the bitter rain. She cried. She cried tears as black as the water in the sky. She let the night fall over her. She listened to the new, dark river below her, which had swept everything away and taken away her grandfather's life. Her grandfather was dead. She was not worried for herself. She was not even surprised or sad. Elena's sorrow was too deep for that.

HEAVEN AND EARTH

She does not see the clouds open up and the starlight break holes in the darkness, the dying moon a crescent wound bleeding light, the winged horse obscured by the mist. She thinks that if she saw them, if she heard the crickets, the coyotes, or felt the frigid wind, it would break her heart. The patterns of stars are fantasies. She huddles against the bleeding warmth of her dead grandfather. She huddles beneath him on a ridge in Wyoming in a place called the Winds. Who am I? she asks. It doesn't matter. The wind is still as cold. The river will yield nothing back. The sky will rain until it is done. Her grandfather is dead. And who she is will change none of it.

"Grandpa," she says. "Grandpa. Grandpa."

And in her mind she hears him. "Go to sleep," he says. "First rest. In the morning we will start again."

The sun broke wickedly bright on the new day. The blue sky already hung with vultures. Her grandfather was cold. She thought to go back down the hill to retrieve the food pack and bridle, but the river had taken the bottom of the ridge. It stretched broadly for a mile to the foot of the mountains where the road once ran out of the hills. It was brown and serene.

She took the canteen from her grandfather's belt, the rifle from his stiffened shoulder. In death, his jaw had reset and his brows lowered. He looked determined again. His eyes, which last night were glassy and lost, were focused and soft. He looked like a man contemplating a lovely but puzzling thing.

She closed his eyes and kissed his forehead. "Good-bye, Grandpa," she said. "I love you. Good-bye."

She had the gun and water. A little hard-tack and jerky in her pockets. The rain had stopped. The horses would come to the high plateau. Her stallion would go to the horses. And she would go to him.

She marked the sun from where it rose and traced its apex across the southern sky. She put that spot on her back. If she remembered correctly, the plateau was almost due north. She was still very wet, and she calculated that it could take her two or three days to reach the meadow on foot, even if she stopped for nothing. But in the late afternoon she rested at a stand of aspen and scrub to strip off her clothes and let them dry in the sun. It warmed her, too, and she sat there, almost thoughtless. First, get your clothes dry. She was still exhausted from the rain and cold, her exertion, trauma, and the two days without sleep. Last night on the ridge did little to replenish her. She

ate a little of the jerky, which tasted salty and miraculous. It made her gums hunger and her stomach
growl for more, so she drank. She might need to find
more water, and she would have to hunt. She would
never find the horse if she did not have the strength,
and she could not take another night of rain and cold.

She walked another hour, giving herself enough
light to search for wood and make camp in the bank
of a hill that protected her from the northwest wind.
She saw then what little she had. No hatchet. She was
forced to burn kindling and antelope scats with some
scraps of dead wood. The sun had dried the lighter
material enough that she got a fire started and dried
out the heavier pieces in sequence of size. Keeping the
fire took all her attention, but she realized as she nib-
bled on her scraps of jerky and hardtack that she had
very little food and had seen no animals during the
day but small birds. She knew how to shoot and skin
an animal, and in the past it had seemed easy. As if by
accident she and her grandfather flushed game from
the chaparral with their horses, surprising them with
their size and speed. Now she was small and slow.
Animals could smell her, see her coming, and run from
her or hide. The alternative, of course, would be to sit
and wait like a cat, but she did not know where to
wait or how long she could wait. She needed water
and she needed to find the horse.

She slept hard until dawn. Ate and drank a little
and then struck out again. Now the mountain sun became as cruel as the rain, and the shadeless prairie that
stretched under the foothills seemed featureless and
endless. The sun ran across the blue-yellow sky without direction, and by afternoon she was convinced
that she was lost. Every landmark she had set for herself looked farther away. Each clump of brush and
chaparral that she marked at the top of one hill van-

ished when she reached the next. Her food would be gone that night and her water was diminishing. If she knew where she was, she'd walk for the little stream she used to visit in the afternoon with her stallion, where he grazed and she sat and dreamed, but she felt that to strike out in a new direction would be even more senseless than continuing on.

That night, before sleeping, she walked away from the fire and gazed up at the sky. It seemed ablaze with vibrating stars, frightening in its color and fullness. So bright, so prolific, that her familiar constellations, the swan, the eagle, the bowman, the scorpion, her winged horse, disappeared in the spray of light.

She dreamed that her stallion stood over the next hill, denying her, punishing her with his distance. In the daylight he walked at an illusive pace, a minute ahead of her sight. She thought in her dream that if she did not find food or water by the end of the next night, then she would not stop tracking him when it grew dark, but she would walk night and day toward the mountains until she found him.

But it was only a dream. And if it was only a dream, she said out loud when she awoke in the dawn, then why do I smell him in the breeze?

The next day she walked in the high desert of her regret. Only a week ago she had been an innocent and foolish girl, full with her own selfish future. Now she was something else. What had her grandfather said? That knowledge was everything, and that knowledge ruined paradise. She wondered, as the day ended, her food gone, her water so low that she began only to rinse her mouth with the final droplets, spitting half of the water and saliva back into the canteen, she wondered if she would die. If she had a pencil and paper, she would leave a note. She'd write a letter to her grandma and grandpa, her mother and father. She would say, *I'm sorry and I love you.* And she would die out here. They would find her and her note would say, *I love you. Love me. It is not your fault.* Though it would accomplish little or nothing. She felt now that she knew something about sorrow.

A movement behind some scrub broke her remorse. It was almost evening, the high desert unchanging in the flattening light, when she saw the rattler. She could not sleep with him there near her and she did not know if she could find another ledge against the wind before dark. She walked up to him, keeping a distance of about ten feet. He'd be looking for a warm place to sleep, which could mean her death. She was looking for food.

The snake stopped when he saw her. He was a thick, old rattlesnake, a good four feet long with a huge triangular head, his rattle the size of her index finger. His skin was dark and full of diamonds that shone in the slanting sunlight like polished leather. He was not afraid. He was cautious. He lay still, watching. He waited.

She was not close enough that he needed to rear up. He lay on his belly quietly, now motionless. She was too big to eat, but he could strike in a blink to defend himself. She saw the snake like a blade of grass, like the hair of the goddess earth or Medusa's head. She released the safety on her rifle. She raised it, drew a bead on his head, and shot him.

She waited for him to stop writhing. She watched him a long, long time before walking over and cutting off the bloody head with her buck knife. She was still afraid enough of his poison to cut a good four inches down, but too hungry to give up any more meat. She did not know where he made his poison, but if she died by eating him, she could die by being afraid to eat him, too. She made a fire, skinned him, took the meat from his bones. She took the unused part of the carcass, his skin, his guts and bones, and returned it to the pool of his blood, to the blood-stained ground where his head lay, and placed it there. She thanked him for his life. Then she roasted his meat piece by piece on a stick over her fire.

In the morning she awoke to the sound of his thunder. He stood with his front hooves in the pool of blood, on the carcass of the snake. He was huge, and the heat rose like steam from his back in the cold morning air. Behind him the full moon set against the prairie. He raised a leg as if to play with its light, as if the moon were something to step on before flying.

She slung the rifle over her head and hooked the canteen to her belt, then walked to the stallion. He sniffed her hand, her face. His throat rumbled with desire. She took his mane and in a moment was upon him.

He did not hesitate, but broke for the sky. Up and up, between the setting moon and the rising sun. Toward the mountaintops. He ran. She did not ride him. He ran with her. She ran with him. Through the morning, as the sun climbed, she clung to his back in timeless running. Then, she did not know if the day passed, if the night passed, or how many days and nights passed as they ran. She felt as if they ran across the sky, nothing above them or below them, and only the constant thundering of his hooves, the roll of his shoulders, the push of his breath.

When they broke into the meadow the herd rose to him. They began to circle as the yellow horse surrounded them, running against their swirl like a centrifuge. They spun. Like the arms of a galaxy they spun. Then he whirled back upon the herd, leading them now in a string of motion toward the high pass above the meadow. In the pack of stampeding mares and foals she spotted her grandfather's sorrels, running together under the sun.

The herd followed him through the pass, farther into the sky, until they came to another high canyon, where he circled them until they came to rest and fed again on the grass. Finally then, he walked to a stream, where she dismounted and they both drank.

Elena gazed at this heaven. How long could she run with this stallion, these horses? Forever. She turned to the stallion, who again came to her, and again she was upon him. He galloped out, again circling the herd. Then he left them. He slowed and trotted through a grove of pines until he came upon a wall of granite, which he followed to a tight opening in the cliffs. Then he walked, entering the wedge, following a rocky path that ascended through the narrow cliffs like stairs. The wind whistled through the gray passageway, which hung with shadows and lichen, a wall of dusk broken only by the sliver of blue sky directly above them. One of the cliffs fell away, and now they walked upon a ledge, the sky falling out from underneath them. Then, around a turn, the other cliff fell away, too, and there was nothing but a narrow path that hung in the sky over the abyss of the Continental Divide. There the stallion walked on air, his sweating back the only thing between the girl and flying.

He took her up and up until the ledge widened and he burst out onto a plateau that opened into the sky, above the mountains, above the air, above everything. They ran. There, together alone, the two of them ran.

Then she saw, as he ran and ran, that he had turned them to the mountains again that rose still higher. She did not know how far he would run with her, where he would leave her, but if this were the line between her old life and death, then she would ride it as if it were the last sacrament. She leaned forward on her horse and whispered to him. "You can take me," she whispered into his running. "I will go where you go. You can take me anywhere." And the stallion burst out again with blinding speed, for the sun, for the stars, for mountains higher than heaven and canyons deeper than the soul.

As the dusk came he stopped at a grove at the edge of the plateau, a small descent to where the silver mountain peaks rose up yet again. There was a small stream and the last stand of pines before the land went up beyond the tree line. The stallion stopped, and in the twilight she saw some boulders, and behind them an opening in the mountain wall just beyond the trees. She petted the animal's neck. "You want me to rest here," she said, and she dismounted.

She walked behind the boulders to the cave and went inside. There, she found an embossed saddle and breast collar, a saddle blanket, a bridle, and saddlebags. On the back of the cantle, engraved on a silver plate, the name, *Elena Estrellas*.

In the saddlebags she found a tube of red lipstick and a makeup compact made of blue-green turquoise stone, the color of the grass and sky. It was the shape of an oyster shell and trimmed in silver. Elena ran her hands over the compact. She thought it was the most beautiful thing she had ever seen. Inside was the mirror where she found her own image, and the beige powder that her grandmother had put on her face, applying lipstick and makeup for her meeting with death.

In the other bag Elena found a silver belt buckle carved with the image of a barrel racer. Over the top it said, *Elena Estrellas*. Across the bottom, *Five Times World Champion*.

And she found a letter in a sealed envelope.

Elena looked out from the cave to the stallion, who stood in the miraculous twilight of the setting sun and rising moon, which now, not quite full, carried the first crescent shadow of its turning. She placed the buckle and makeup back in the bags and carried the letter from the cave where she broke the seal and opened the message to read it in the moonlight.

Dear Joe,

I can't imagine anyone else finding this. And I know you're mad I didn't let you keep me company till the end. But dying is something you do alone, Joe. You can't go where I'm going. Not yet. And you won't find my remains around here, so don't look. I flew away. Think of me next to you (you sweat in bed, do you know that? I always told you I liked you sweaty, but I lied). Think of me riding. You're a sweet lover, Joe. A good man.

You'd think somebody's last written words would be more profound. Anyway, I always thought you were the profound one. Too much time in Japan. It made you more religious than spiritual. So you probably think this is the end of me, while I think I'm just crossing over. When I see you again, my love, you'll look at me and once again know that I was right and you were wrong. Death won't have changed a damn thing. Never does.

I love you so much, Joe. I love you. I hope you find me in the sun and wind, in the green grass and blue sky, in the trees and chaparral and stars. I want to be the air you breathe and the beating of your heart. I wish I could never leave you. But for now I must die. I cannot choose otherwise. I must die now. Love me and forgive me enough to have let me die this way.

Tell Gala (or whatever she's calling herself now) that I love her. Tell Harlan to get a job. Tell that little cowgirl, Elena, that she's named after me, and every time I got thrown, I got better. If the stallion ever comes back to you, if she wants, she can have him. Tell the moon and stars you're mine, Joe. This letter is my ashes. Tear it up and give it to the wind.

Adios, my love,
Your Elena of the Stars

She dared not sleep because she did not know how long the horse would wait for her. As Pegasus emerged from the darkness, flying above the moon, she placed the blanket on the stallion, and then her grandmother's racing saddle. She cinched the saddle and fastened the breast collar, then offered the stallion the bit, easing the bridle over his ears. She fastened it. Walked him. Then tightened the cinch when he let out his wind. She left the saddlebags with the compact and lipstick in the cave, but kept the letter in her hand. Finally, grabbing his mane, she mounted the stallion. She turned him, then tore her grandmother's letter and released it to the wind.

She rode through the night. Over the plateau and across the backbone ridge that now, in the darkness, put her amid the stars themselves. Back down through the narrow gully and into high meadow.

Now the horse began to fly, but she eased him back to a fast canter, which was still ten times faster than her walking. Once down from the second meadow and into the prairie, he knew his way and ran it straight. She rode all night. She gave him the rein and flew with him out of the night and into the dawn.

With the sun coming up over the mountains, they ran for the ridge above the ranch. She reached it under the morning light. Under the new sun she saw that the river had receded, though it left nothing of her grandfather's cabin or barn. Where her grandfather once lay dead, she saw the parallel tracks of a helicopter, the chaparral blown back from the propeller wind. In the distance she heard the machine lopping in the sky, and across the way, where the river had gone down, on a barren island above the ranch, she saw the camp, the tents, the huge rubber raft, the ravaged dirt of the helicopter pad. Farther down, trucks and cars parked on the muddy road below the mountains. But at the camp, she saw her parents near the campfire.

Her mother was the first to see the girl and the horse, her hands going into the air. The girl could hear her yell, "Elena! Elena!" Without seeing she saw the tears in her mother's eyes. She saw her father's hands drop to his sides, then he ran to her mother.

She waved. As her parents ran to the raft, she dismounted. She uncinched the saddle and breast collar and took the saddle and blanket from the stallion. She pulled the bridle down and let the bit fall from his mouth.

"Go," she said to him. "Go."

The animal leaped away without hesitation, running back to the hills, his tail raised above him in a question mark. She put the bridle and reins over her shoulder and folded the blanket under the same arm. She lifted the saddle by the horn and pulled it onto her back. Elena turned for home.